CLAIRE DALTON

◆

TAKE A CHANCE ON LOVE

Complete and Unabridged

LINFORD
Leicester

First published in Great Britain in 2010

First Linford Edition
published 2011

British Library CIP Data

Dalton, Claire.
 Take a chance on love. - -
 (Linford romance library)
 1. Newspaper employees- -Fiction.
 2. Love stories.
 3. Large type books.
 I. Title II. Series
 823.9'2–dc22

 ISBN 978–1–4448–0631–1

Published by
F. A. Thorpe (Publishing)
Anstey, Leicestershire

Words & Graphics Ltd.
Anstey, Leicestershire
Printed and bound in Great Britain by
T. J. International Ltd., Padstow, Cornwall

This book is printed on acid-free paper

TAKE A CHANCE ON LOVE

After returning to her home town, Catherine Earnshaw plans to spend all her time on her job at the local newspaper and caring for her elderly father. One thing she's sure of is that there's no room for a man in her new life. She's been hurt once before and she daren't allow herself to fall for the enigmatic Sean Bradford-Jones, or rely on him when all her plans start to unravel . . .

An Emotional Return

'Oh, come on!' Catherine Earnshaw tapped her hand impatiently on the steering wheel as she watched the truck slowly reverse across the road. Wasn't this what she'd wanted to leave behind in London? Surely there shouldn't be any traffic on a small-town road at this time on a dark, misty evening?

Straining to look at the truck's painstaking progress through the deepening gloom, she noticed the first drops of rain on the windscreen. It was getting worse. A wild, stormy night on the edge of the moors . . .

She closed her eyes and thought about what it *should* be like. If her life was a Victorian novel, this would be when the hero appeared. He would emerge out of the mist, tall, dark and brooding — angry at the elements, angry at the unfairness of the world and most of all angry at herself, the heroine, though that anger would be combined with an overwhelming attraction which would inevitably lead to passionate, eternal, all-consuming love . . .

The sound of someone knocking on the driver's window brought her back down to earth with a resounding bump.

'Oh!' Down to earth that was, until she looked at the face watching her through the rain-spattered glass.

He knocked again and without thinking she pressed the button to lower the window. 'Hey there,' he said, but Catherine just stared at him.

He could have been tall — he was bending down to speak through the car window — but he definitely wasn't dark. Nor was he brooding or angry, because he was smiling at her in way that belied his next words. 'Sorry about this,' he said without a trace of apology in his voice. 'The truck will be out of the way in a moment.'

A few drops of rain found their way into the car and the effect was the same as the coldest, heaviest shower. What was she doing — gaping at some man from a building site who was delaying her journey home, and all because he happened to appear at the moment she was lost in that silly adolescent fantasy . . .

She blinked once or twice. 'What's going on?' she asked sharply, her gaze slipping beyond him to the slowly moving truck.

His eyes followed her gaze. 'They're making a delivery.'

'At this time of night?'

'Only time they could do it,' he said, turning back to her with amusement on his face.

I wonder why, she thought waspishly. 'This is very inconvenient,' she said pettily and was even more annoyed when the amusement on his face developed into a broad smile — at her expense.

'I'm sure you have somewhere very important to go . . . Miss. I'll get you on your way as soon as possible. Trust me.'

Get her on her way? Trust him?

She'd sooner walk back to Holly Cottage than rely on this stranger for anything at all and she opened her mouth to tell him so, but at that moment the truck suddenly disappeared into the darkness beyond the road, leaving her way clear at last.

'Thanks, Ed,' the man called out then he turned his attention back to Catherine. 'I said you could trust me. All clear now — off you go.'

With that he straightened and tapped a hand on the car roof to signal her departure before strolling away towards his building site. Well, of all the nerve . . . She watched him walk away, without a backward glance, and she noticed that he was in fact tall. That his shoulders were broad and although he was dressed for manual work, he walked with an easy grace. Swallowing nervously, she turned her attention back to the car, began to release the clutch and promptly stalled the engine.

What was the matter with her? She *never* stalled the car, never had any trouble keeping her composure, yet here she was ... Glancing down she fumbled with the key in the ignition, and finally the engine burst back into life. Resolutely she kept her eyes focussed on the road, but somehow she knew the man had stopped and was watching her as she drove away. No way was she going to look at him, look into those blue eyes, or at those well-formed lips.

Listen to yourself, Catherine Earnshaw, she told herself severely. Still having that ridiculous daydream at your age? For heaven's sake. You're not a heroine in a Victorian novel, despite your name, and there is no storybook hero out there ready to sweep you off your feet. So stop waiting for him. He doesn't exist and even if there were such a man, you did not leave London in the expectation of finding him here in a Yorkshire seaside town.

He wasn't bad-looking in a builder-labourer sort of way, she thought with a scowl.

It was a cliché, the kind she avoided at all costs in her work — the ruggedly attractive manual worker with a twinkle in his eye and the cheek of the devil in his speech. Good grief, he even had a cheeky Irish accent.

'*There is no such thing as a cliché, Miranda*', her first editor in London, had proclaimed on so many occasions that the statement had become a cliché in itself. And Miranda had been wrong. There were clichés everywhere and the man she'd just encountered could have been conjured up in the imagination of half the women she'd ever worked with, let alone their thousands of female readers.

Trying to put the encounter out of her mind, she parked carefully beside her father's, now rarely used, small hatchback. It ought to be sold, she thought vaguely as she started to unload her shopping. Now she was home she would do the driving. She didn't really like the thought of her father being behind the wheel anymore, though she couldn't tell him that.

'Dad, I'm back,' she called, carrying the first two bags into the kitchen and setting them down on the table.

She made several trips back to the car before she was finished and could lock the front door behind her, brushing the raindrops from her dark brown hair as she re-entered the kitchen. The kitchen had always been the heart of their home and her father was waiting there, gazing in astonishment at the pile of groceries on the table.

'However much did you get, Katie?' Bill Earnshaw asked as she started to unpack the white plastic bags.

Katie. Her dad had used the nickname for as long as she could remember, despite her mother's protestations. His use of it now conjured up images from the past and Catherine felt a pang as she thought of her mother and how much she still missed her. 'Home' wasn't quite the sanctuary it had seemed in the days when Ann

Earnshaw was there to welcome and comfort her. Sometimes she just wanted someone to talk to . . .

But she didn't want to upset her dad. He was finding it hard enough coming to terms with his own grief without his daughter adding to it. She had to be the strong one so she shrugged and said easily, 'There's two of us to feed now I'm home, Dad.'

'I have been eating,' he said slightly testily, and Catherine turned to smile at him as she shoved packets of pasta into a wall cupboard. She wasn't so sure that he did eat when he was here in Holly Cottage all alone, but she wasn't going to say so out loud.

'I know you have. I just got carried away, that's all.'

'And all at nine o'clock at night! Why would anyone want to go shopping at this time of night?'

Catherine laughed at the expression on her father's face, wrinkled now behind the large glasses and beneath the thatch of snow-white hair. 'Twenty-four hour shopping comes to Bridby!'

He shook his head and started to help her unpack the groceries. She let him — it wasn't an arduous task so there was no need to worry about his physical strength for once. She didn't know what was worse — the thought of her father behind the wheel of a car, or walking back to the cottage carrying heavy bags . . .

'Sorry I was so long,' she said casually. 'I was delayed on the way back — some man decided to block the road with a delivery of something that looked very dodgy.'

'Dodgy?'

'Who has a delivery to a building site at night? Anyway, I had to wait to get past.'

'There's a lot of building going on in the town,' her father commented. 'Extensions, or people putting a room over their garages. There's always something going on. Then there's all the plans for the site on the cliffs. That's a bigger thing, mind. It's costing millions.'

'I know. There's a presentation about the plans on Friday that I'm going to. As if there's not enough to do at the newspaper, but you know how it is.'

'The editor of the Gazette is an important person in Bridby.' He paused for a moment and his voice was softer when he spoke again. 'They'll get used to you, love.'

Catherine ran her hands through her hair, still slightly damp from the rain. It was straight and fell just to her chin which meant it was normally easy to take care of, unless it was wet. 'I know they will,' she said quietly, leaning back against the table as she faced him. 'It's only my first week — right now they're creeping around me, when they're forgetting to resent me, that is. They think I'm some high-flying editor from London who wants to change everything they do.'

'They're lucky to have you — though why you would want to come to back to this little town and move in with your old dad I don't know. You should be out and about with a young man, dancing and what-not.'

'Oh, Dad. You make me sound like a young girl.'

'You are a young girl to me.'

Catherine found herself smiling as she handed him the magazine she had bought especially at the supermarket. It wasn't the sort of magazine she could imagine editing, but she knew it was very popular with elderly people, which is exactly what her dad was. Elderly — and for the past three years alone. Until now . . . 'Your eyes must be going, along with everything else,' she said cheekily, knowing he would respond to her teasing.

'I'm not quite past it yet, Katie.' He took off his glasses and waved them in her direction in a vague gesture of admonishment that reminded her of her childhood. 'I have my crosswords and my local history course. And I'm playing chess again now I've found a fellow enthusiast. I don't need you lecturing me on taking it easy as well.'

'Who else has been lecturing you?' she asked with a grin, but he did not reply because he'd already slipped his glasses back on to his nose and was turning away to take his new reading material into the sitting room.

Catherine watched him go with amused affection. What would she do without her dad? It was the second time this evening that she'd watched a man walk away from her but the sight of her father was very different from that of the labourer she'd encountered on the road. She could see it in every bone in his body, in the way he held himself, the way he moved.

When had he become an old man, she wondered, her smile fading. She saw him often enough but somehow he had aged without her realising it. Seventy wasn't really old these days, but she could see the change in him. It's just high blood pressure, she'd told herself over and over again. High blood pressure and the passage of time. You couldn't stop that, or even slow it down.

She sighed and opened one of the cupboards, reaching for the tea caddy. Cup of tea or glass of wine? Both, she decided. For some reason she was in a reflective mood tonight. Maybe it was the weather, the way the wind was rattling the windows, blowing the rain against the glass. Maybe it was because she knew it would take a while for the staff of the newspaper to 'get used to her'. Maybe it was because she didn't know anyone in Bridby anymore. Maybe it was because suddenly she felt very alone.

She turned to the window and looked out into the swirling darkness. Sixteen years ago she'd left this small coastal town on the edge of the moors in search of a dream. Dreams, really, and some of them had come true, just as others hadn't. The naïve teenager who had left Bridby that day looked out at her from a photograph in the hallway, just as her four-year-old self watched her, wide-eyed, in the sitting room, and the new graduate looked out proudly from beneath a cap and gown in the dining room.

It all seemed like a long time ago and so much had happened. Wonderful things that she would never have dared to imagine, then things that weren't so good. That 18-year-old girl was a stranger to the woman she had become because 16 years of living separated them. She could barely recognise herself in that ambitious adolescent, and she was not sure she wanted to.

But she still had some yearnings. That was why she'd allowed herself that silly fantasy earlier in the evening. For a few glorious moments the man of her dreams had been standing in front of her. After all these years.

★   ★   ★

'I'm thirty-four and on the shelf. I'll never meet anyone and I'm going to be on my own forever.'

Helen Padley had laughed out loud at Catherine's words and protested in her soft local accent. 'On the shelf? Your life's like something on TV compared to mine, Catherine. I've got three kids and a husband who works twelve hours a day, while you've been editing a brilliant women's magazine.'

Catherine shook her head and smiled to herself as she let herself into Holly Cottage once more and shot the bolt across. She wouldn't be going out again tonight so she could lock up and relax. And think about the day she'd just had.

The hours reading page proofs before they went to press were hard work but it had been a good day. Her very first edition of the newspaper was printed — and she'd made a new friend. Well, an old friend actually because the blonde, slightly plump woman who'd appeared at her office door had turned out to be not only the Gazette's part-time feature writer but her own teenage friend from school. Helen Danielson as was, now Helen Padley.

'You work for the Gazette?' she'd asked in astonishment.

'I work for you — now you're the editor.'

Yeah, she was the editor . . . She'd edited Élan magazine for three years, but this was different — the Bridby Gazette was her home-town newspaper and she was beginning to realise the challenge it represented. Her dream job . . . So she'd read every page carefully, several times, the end result being an immaculate edition of the Gazette and a headache and a stiff neck for herself.

Flinging her briefcase on to the hall chair, she paused for a moment. She could hear voices from the sitting room, presumably her father watching TV. Probably one of the antiques pro-grammes he enjoyed so much, she thought with a smile. As if they would find anything more than dry rot, or rising damp, in their own attic!

'Just me, Dad,' she called as she slipped off her shoes. 'I'm exhausted so I'm going to take a bath. I won't be long.' She heard a muffled reply as she headed for the stairs, but she didn't wait to disturb him. She'd tell him about Helen later.

It was nice, having someone to come home to, she thought stretching out among the lavender scented bubbles. How long had she lived alone in London? It must be, she counted back, seven years since Peter had left her for another woman. She'd never wanted to marry anyone else after that. She become used to her routine, her space and she was always so busy at the office that the peace and solitude her flat offered had seemed like heaven.

Anyway, her dad needed her. He was the focus of her attention — he and the Gazette. She didn't need anything else. A hero of her own . . . Maybe, but they weren't easy to come by, were they?

'We could do a feature on my husband. He runs his own garage but he's also one of the senior crew of the Bridby lifeboat,' Helen Padley had suggested as she sat on one of the newly delivered sofas in Catherine's office, sipping a cup of coffee from the shiny, state-of-the-art espresso and cappuccino machine.

An idea had stirred in Catherine's mind. The lifeboat station was such an important aspect of life the town and the men and women who volunteered regularly risked their lives to help others . . . 'Really?' she said thoughtfully.

'There's so much going on there,' Helen had said. 'All sorts of people are involved. Like the architect of the new development on the cliff. He'd probably be able to tell you more about the lifeboat than my Dave. He's very good-looking, too.'

A handsome rescuer? Catherine had a flash of memory of the man she'd encountered on the road the night before. He had certainly been very good-looking and she'd cast him in the role of romantic hero for those few brief moments before he'd disappeared into the night. She still wasn't convinced she hadn't dreamt the whole thing . . .

'Do you remember all those Victorian

novels we used to read?' Helen had asked with a grin as if she could read Catherine's thoughts. 'We were going to wait for our own hero who'd sweep us off our feet just like Mr Rochester. And here's me, married for fourteen years to a bloke I went to school with. Are you married?'

'No.' Catherine did not know what else to say. That question always seemed to require some sort of explanation.

'That's why you're the editor and I'm not,' Helen had said practically, saving her the trouble.

Yes, that was why she was the editor and that was why she was thirty-four and single. Put like that it didn't sound so bad and she smiled to herself as she sank deeper into the fragrant bath water.

Warm and relaxed, eventually she wandered down to the kitchen. Holly Cottage might have seen better days but the central heating was surprisingly efficient. They could do with a new kitchen though, she thought as she filled the kettle. Her father probably didn't notice. How long had he lived in at the cottage? Thirty-nine years — since before she was born.

And I think this fridge has been here for every one of those years, Catherine thought with a wry smile. That would be next on the list to update. If only her solicitor could speed up the sale of the flat in London . . .

She had a vague itch on the back of one ankle and absent-mindedly raised the other foot to rub against it. As she was thinking about how the musty old carpet really had to replaced by something more modern, such as ceramic tiles, she heard the door open and someone enter the kitchen.

'Have you had a cup of tea already, Dad?' she asked casually as she reached up for the caddy.

There was the shortest of silences then . . . 'I'm afraid we've been on something stronger.'

How she didn't drop the wretched caddy or pull the whole cupboard off the wall she would never know. First of all, the voice that had answered her wasn't her father's. And if that weren't enough, it bore the unmistakeable lilt of the northern part of Ireland . . .

She swung around and her eyes widened at the sight of him, even more shocking than the sound of his voice. He was even taller than she had thought and in the soft light of the single kitchen lamp his hair had golden hues intermingled with the dark blond. He wore jeans again, this time with a thin sweater that clung to the muscles of his broad chest, and he was free of the grime and dust of the building site. He was also absolutely, undeniably, unbelievably handsome.

And he was standing in her kitchen as if he owned it.

Catherine Meets Her Father's Friend

'What on earth are you doing here?' she asked, even to her own ears her voice sounding strained.

She prided herself on her calmness whatever the occasion or provocation, but there was something about the way this man was standing in her kitchen gazing at her. And she, Catherine realised, was dressed in her oldest and tattiest pyjamas.

'I'm playing chess with your dad.'

He was her father's new friend. He'd said he was playing the game again but had never told her who with. 'You play chess with Dad?'

He folded his arms across his chest and watched her with amused eyes. 'Who did you think he was playing chess with?'

It was a perfectly reasonable question

but not one Catherine knew how to answer. She could hardly say 'some old man with white hair and a walking stick', could she?

Just as at their previous encounter, she could sense that he knew exactly what she was thinking, exactly how uncomfortable he was making her, and that he was finding the whole situation highly amusing. 'How often do you play chess here?' she asked with a frown.

He seemed to think for a moment. 'Once a week.'

'And how long has this been going on?'

'About . . . ' he glanced down at his watch, lifting one wrist to do so, 'One hour and ten minutes.'

She deserved that. Against all her intentions she looked away, but she didn't need to see him to know that this man — this mysterious, disturbing man — was watching her.

'I know you're some high-flying London journalist but if you want to interview me, can I have that hot drink you were offering before you start?' he said in that slow drawl that seemed to set nerves tingling. 'That's what Bill sent me to ask . . . '

She swallowed nervously and tried to remember where she was, who she was. *I can't imagine any occasion when I would want to interview you,* she thought but thankfully stopped herself from saying it out loud. She had to keep herself together here because there was really no reason to be so ill at ease. You're not a silly young girl, she told herself severely, so stop acting like one.

'That's what I was about to do,' she said with forced lightness as she turned away. 'I wasn't expecting a guest, but . . . OK, we have tea, coffee, hot chocolate or I have camomile and peppermint. They're herbal teas, by the way,' she added helpfully.

She glanced at him just in time to catch the amusement on his face. 'Thanks for the explanation,' he said calmly. 'I'll have ordinary, common tea. With milk but no sugar. That's the white stuff some people put into their drink to sweeten it.'

She felt a warmth in her cheeks and cursed herself silently. Blushing was one of the annoying habits she'd never managed to rid herself of, along with that irritating tendency to interview everyone she met rather than simply talk to them. She tried to hide her embarrassment by concentrating on the three mugs in front of her. 'Fine. Tell Dad I'll bring them through.'

She felt his surprise and the slight hesitation before he turned on his heels and left her alone. Catherine let out a deep breath and hung her head even lower.

Her heart was pounding and she couldn't have said why except that he was the most attractive man she'd ever met. Suddenly he'd gone from being a mysterious stranger she would never see again into someone who would be a regular presence in her home. And she didn't know if she was appalled or excited by the prospect.

She glanced down at her old pyjamas. Instinct told her to rush upstairs and at least pull on some sweatpants or jeans, but she could imagine the look in those piercing blue eyes if she did so.

Piercing blue eyes. That was another cliche but she didn't seem to be able to avoid them where this man was concerned. He had barely spoken to her yet he had haunted her dreams in the way that only fictional heroes had done before.

You are thirty-four, she told herself. You have never dressed for a man and you are not going to start now. This is your home and you will wear whatever you want. He's probably married with kids anyway, so what does it matter what he thinks of you?

A few minutes later she carried a tray bearing three mugs and a book into the sitting room. It took every ounce of her control to walk across the room, knowing her every step was being followed by that man's interested eyes as well as her father's kindly ones.

'Hello, love,' Bill Earnshaw said cheerfully as she set the tray down on the table. 'Have you had a busy night?'

'Mmm, yes. It will be like this every Thursday.' She put one mug down in front of her father and another in front of the stranger.

'Is the newspaper printed?'

'It is. My first!'

Bill Earnshaw smiled at her and Catherine felt a wave of affection for her father that drove out any other thoughts. It hadn't been easy for him since her mother's death and it was good to see him looking happy again. She'd worried about him so much when they were hundreds of miles apart, and she was glad she'd come home.

'You've met Sean?' he was saying brightly and irresistibly her gaze was drawn to the man seated opposite him at the table.

Sean. That was his name, then. 'Yes. We've met,' she said quickly, forestalling any introduction.

'He's not a bad chess player, Katie. He's even beaten me once or twice.'

'Once or twice?'

Sean looked up and a smile curved across those beautifully-shaped lips. 'He's a mean chess player, your dad,' he said with humour. 'I was taken in at first.'

She found herself responding to his smile. 'Don't be. Beneath that harmless exterior beats the heart of a Mississippi gambler.'

'I know!'

Picking up her own drink, Catherine crossed over to her favourite armchair. She'd decided she wasn't going to run, and actually it seemed as if she didn't have to because both Sean and her father turned their attention back to the chessboard in front of them.

She curled up in the chair, tucking her legs beneath her, and opened her book. It was one her favourites — one of the novels she and Helen Danielson had read while perched on the window seat of her room. And she let her mind wander back across the years to those long Sunday afternoons when instead of concentrating on their homework they let themselves be taken to another world by the storytellers they loved.

With the rain streaming down the window, they had allowed themselves to be seduced by Heathcliff, Mr Rochester, Mr Darcy, and they'd had their first dreams of romantic love . . .

From across the room, her father's guest watched her as she read. It was one advantage of chess, the game was slow enough to allow his attention to wander slightly without it attracting his opponent's notice.

He'd known who she was the moment he saw her in the car, all glossy dark hair and smoky grey eyes that a man could lose himself in if he allowed it to happen. He'd seen enough pictures of Bill Earnshaw's daughter — as a child, teenager, woman — to recognise her straightaway, despite the gloom, despite the scowl on her face and despite the frosty greeting.

Yes, he'd recognised her, but the real woman was nothing like the sophisticated girl-about-about-town pictured in her even more sophisticated magazine. He'd always disliked those magazines and had only looked at them in deference to his friend's natural pride in his daughter, though for some reason he'd found himself reading every word Catherine had written . . .

In the dim light of the road he hadn't been able to see her clearly but he was seeing more of her now. And she didn't like him. That in itself was enough to intrigue him because it wasn't something he was used to. He knew how women reacted to him and much as it bored him, there was nothing he could do about it. But Catherine Earnshaw was different to the vacuous females who smiled and flirted and tried to capture his attention.

She'd taken one look at him and made a whole range of assumptions that made her dislike him even more.

Which could have made him dislike her, despite her obvious beauty, except that she'd blushed when he looked at her.

He looked at her and noticed the way her hair curled under slightly at the ends. She seemed very conscious of her hair, that dark hair with the expensive cut, and every so often her hand would move to twirl one strand round and round her index finger as she read.

Then the next moment she would tuck the same strand behind her ear where it would stay for a few moments till her restless hand would free it once more so it hung loose and heavy against her cheek.

'Do you play chess?' he asked, and he watched as she raised her head to look at him. For a moment, there was confusion in her clear grey eyes, as if she had forgotten his presence so engrossed was she in her book.

She blinked, once, then twice, before smiling vaguely in his direction. 'No.'

'Didn't you join the chess club at

school, Katie?' Bill asked.

'That was only because I fancied Michael Bellamy,' she said matter-of-factly. 'Then I discovered how boring both he and chess were.'

'Not enough action for you?'

He heard her father chuckle but it was the flicker of emotion in her eyes that intrigued him even more, before she resolutely returned her gaze to her book.

That had been her thought exactly, Catherine reflected in wry amusement. She had wanted Michael Bellamy to admire her, to kiss her, yet all he had been interested in was the strategy of the rook, knight, pawn and queen . . . That had been the only thing that attracted her about the whole game, she remembered — that the queen was dominant in it all.

She shook her head slightly and focussed her eyes on the text before her. She was enjoying re-reading the story of Jane Eyre, though she had been convinced she would never be able to concentrate with that man in the room.

There was something quite comforting about the whole scene, she mused as she contemplated the literary heroine's own vision of perfect happiness. At the table, her father and his new friend continued their game, speaking only occasionally as the game demanded, but engrossed in both the challenge and each other's company. Her dad was comfortable with the man he'd introduced as 'Sean' and this must be just the latest of many evening games of chess they had shared over a glass of whisky.

She lifted her head to look at the stranger her father seemed to trust so much. For some reason it was his forearms that her eyes sought out. Maybe it was because they were resting on the table as he contemplated his next move. His arms . . . There was a light dusting of fair hair, just the right amount. They looked sinewy, too. It would be the physical work every day spent on a building site, physical labour in direct contrast to everything she'd ever known.

He'd probably done it for years. He must be in his mid-30s. She watched as he leant forward to pick up one of the chess pieces. His hands were large but surprisingly shapely with long fingers that seemed to caress the knight as he prepared to make a move that he hoped would leave him in an unassailable position, make the winning of the game a foregone conclusion . . .

She forced her attention back to the here and now, and listened for a moment to the casual conversation between her father and his new friend as they continued their chess game.

'You'll be glad the better weather's arrived,' her father commented as he moved one pawn into what was probably a better position though Catherine couldn't really tell.

The man with the beautiful eyes and the seductive accent chuckled softly, and a new assault on her senses began. 'I know. It was no joke living in a caravan during the winter. I can tell you that, Bill.'

OK, this made it easier. Somehow it was so much easier to ignore all the things about him that attracted her if there was something that didn't. 'You live in a caravan?' she asked deliberately.

'Yeah.' Her scepticism must have been written on her face because she saw the flash of amusement in his eyes. 'This is a holiday resort, there's plenty of caravans, if you think about it,' he said.

'For two-week holidays. People stay in them, they don't live in them,' she said tartly, wondering why he could rile her by saying the most reasonable things in the most polite tone of voice. Somehow it only made her all the more edgy and wary of him.

He shrugged and exchanged an amused glance with her father. 'Probably more do than you realise.'

'There's a lot of people living in caravans now, Katie,' her father pointed out eagerly. 'People who have retired here. And the caravans are nothing like the ones you remember from years ago. They have all mod cons now, don't they, Sean?'

'They do. I can cook and wash, though Bill sometimes lets me come over for a bath. As a change from a shower every day after work.'

Suddenly she was no longer interested in her book. Even Mr Rochester had lost his attraction but she used all her powers of concentration and forced herself to read the words. The fact it was the same words over and over again helped because eventually their meaning began to sink in. It was the wrong choice of book, that was the problem, Catherine told herself. She should have read something more prosaic than a tale of repressed passion and hidden longing. She should have read a home interiors magazine. Or maybe the telephone directory.

'Oh look at that!'

She looked up at her father's

36

exclamation. The two men were grinning at each other as the younger of the pair began to drop the chess pieces back into their box, one by one.

'A rare triumph,' Sean said easily as he stood up. 'You must have been distracted tonight, Bill.'

'I think I was. I'm not used to having my Katie back.'

She felt their gaze on her and looked up.

'But I'm very glad she came home,' her father continued and Catherine smiled at him.

'So am I,' she said simply.

There was a short silence, then Sean touched his friend on the arm. 'Ah, you're a lucky man to have a beautiful woman to come home to,' he commented, then he looked around for his black leather jacket which Catherine had noticed was slung carelessly across the sofa. 'I'll be off now. Thanks for the game, Bill. No, it's all right. I'll see myself out.'

He paused for a moment then

glanced at Catherine. 'Nice to meet you. Thanks for the tea.'

'You're welcome.' She didn't say it had been nice to meet him and the next moment he had gone, leaving a silence and an emptiness in his wake that both surprised and confused her.

As she watched her father gather up the tea mugs, Catherine thought about his parting words.

A beautiful woman to come home to. It was the flattering, flirtatious remark of the practised charmer and she didn't like it because it was too obvious. He was so sure of himself in the way that all such men were. And he had made himself at home, too. It was the way he moved in their house, the way he seemed almost part of the rooms, as if he belonged there.

A beautiful woman to come home to. So he wasn't married and there probably weren't children either. Especially not if he lived in a caravan and spent frequent evenings here at Holly Cottage with her father.

Bill Earnshaw chuckled as he put away the folded chessboard. 'I'll have to get my revenge next week,' he commented. 'He plays a good game, Sean does, but I'll have my revenge.'

'Dad, how did you meet that man?' Catherine asked slowly.

He looked up with a frown. 'Sean? In the library in town.'

The library! 'What was he doing there? Sheltering from the rain?' she asked but her father didn't seem to notice her sarcasm.

'He was looking up something about local history, I think. That's what I was doing. It's part of my course at the community centre.'

'Did he speak to you first?'

'I think so. Why?'

She hesitated. 'I was wondering . . . You have to be careful, Dad. What do you know about him?'

From across the room Bill Earnshaw looked at her in dismay. 'Oh, Katie!'

'Dad — listen. What do you know about him, he's not from around here.

You were here in this house, alone, and I know you won't want to hear this, but you're a very easy target if someone wanted . . . '

'No, love,' he interrupted, his expression incredulous as he listened to her warning about his friend. 'That's nonsense. You're not in London now, there's no need to be so suspicious of everyone.'

'Dad . . . '

'No, love,' he repeated firmly. 'It's daft, that's what it is. I've only known Sean a few months but I know a good man when I meet one.'

Catherine watched as he sat down in his armchair and picked up his crossword book. For as long as she could remember his favourite pastimes had been crosswords and chess and it was reassuring that some things would never change.

'You're right. I'm sure you're right,' she said eventually and she crossed the room to stand beside his armchair. He'd already started on a puzzle, cryptic of course, and she smiled as she thought about how he always had to be busy. She knew from where she'd inherited her restless mind, her will to succeed, even if in many other ways they were complete opposites . . .

She bent and pressed a soft kiss to his forehead. 'Thanks, Dad,' she said quietly, not quite sure why she was thanking him except that he deserved it.

And as she retreated to her own armchair to take up her book once more, she thought about his words. *You're right,* she'd told him because she didn't want to upset him, not because she believed it.

Just as she didn't believe that it was her dad who needed to be on guard against the influence of his new friend. No, somehow she knew her dad was the least of her worries where that man was concerned. If only she was as calm and confident as she appeared on the surface. If only she was as strong as everyone thought. If only she didn't need . . .

But she suppressed that thought because she, she'd told herself earlier, was the strong one now. Her mum had been gone almost three years and she was home. Bridby was her life. She had her dad to take care of and a paper to edit.

As she forced her eyes to return to Jane Eyre's story once more she reminded herself of her goals, and the ground rules she had set if she wanted to achieve them. She had to work and take care of her dad — there was no time for anything else.

★   ★   ★

Catherine walked into the conference room with about a minute to spare. No matter how she planned, no matter how often she intended to be more organised, it was always a battle not be late. A battle she normally lost.

But at least this time the presentation hadn't actually started so technically she wasn't late at all, she thought as she picked up her name badge and folder. She glanced down at the words on the front, *Radford-Jones Associates*, and flicked through the pages, barely taking in the designs.

OK, she was ready to hear about this plan for the site on the cliffs. The site needed developing, she knew that, but she wondered what exactly was proposed.

She glanced at her watch, then stepped forward to look at the 3D representation of what was grandly called the Bridby Abbey Conference, Creative Industry and Community Centre. All things to all men, Catherine thought wryly, and of course it looked wonderful as only a bright shiny new plastic model could.

Let's see if reality can live up to the daydream, she thought as she sat down beside someone who was familiar from both the present and her past.

'What do you think of this idea, Mr Andrews?' she asked her father's old friend as she flicked through the folder of information once more.

'Hello, Catherine,' Brian Andrews said with a friendly smile. 'It's very impressive, isn't it? This architect fellow has won lots of awards, they say. We had a presentation on the planning committee but the whole council won't decide till later. This is the first time it's been shown.'

'We're putting it in the Gazette next week,' Catherine said thoughtfully.

'It's time we had something to be proud of in this town,' Councillor Andrews said. 'This fellow knows what he's talking about.'

She turned to the back of the folder, towards the architect's biography and let her eyes skim down the page. Sean Radford-Jones, born in Belfast, studied architecture at Cambridge, increasingly specialising in public buildings, awarded international prizes for designing a library in Cordoba, a museum in Manchester and a multi-function office space in Rotterdam . . .

'I hear he's building his own house in

Bridby in his spare time,' the elderly man beside her was saying. 'Up on Scarlington Road.'

Sean Radford-Jones.

Surely her mysterious stranger couldn't be . . . Catherine closed her eyes for a moment, knowing full well that when she opened them she would know for sure, but she didn't even have to wait that long.

She heard his voice first, despite the noise of the 20 or so people in the room, that distinctive Northern Irish accent that seemed to give every word extra resonance, extra meaning . . .

She opened her eyes and felt her face go bright red. Of course it was him and the shock was so great that she could barely think straight — except that she knew that she had made a monumental fool of herself.

She drew in a deep breath and rested one hand against a burning cheek. What an idiot, what an idiot.

She watched as he spoke to one or two people she vaguely knew, chatting fluently and easily as he stood there, one of the plastic folders in his hands. The scruffy labourer from the road and the casually dressed chess player were gone and in their place was a smart, stylish businessman who didn't even need his designer suit, tailored shirt and elegant tie to draw the attention of everyone in the room. Why hadn't he told her who he was? Why hadn't her father said something, she thought resentfully. And why hadn't she figured it out for herself?

When he started to speak, she started slightly and looked back down at the folder. She listened as he thanked everyone for being there, asked someone to dim the lights then began a short presentation.

'I won't bore you all,' he said casually, as confident and in control of this situation as he was of every other he found himself in. 'I'll say a few words and then if you want to ask me questions. I'll do my best to answer them. Have a look at the plans in the folders, and the model and the site itself, then ask whatever you want to know.'

Glancing at the screen behind him, Sean began to speak about the design that was his pride and joy. He'd worked on it for almost a year and he knew it could be the best thing he had ever done.

It was the reason he was living in this small Yorkshire town of all the places in the world he could choose. Something about the picturesque town with its busy, working harbour and its dramatic cliff-top abbey had caught his interest on those brief visits as he'd prepared his design. Then he'd found the disused building with the amazing view and found himself embarking on his own personal project of creating a home of his own.

His eyes rested on Catherine Earnshaw in the front row of the audience. Somehow he'd known she wouldn't feel the need to hide away from his gaze but still it was good to see her where he couldn't help but look at her. He'd become used to the frown and suspicious gaze, but today he noticed an extra flush on her cheek and he suddenly realised that until moments earlier she had had no idea who he was.

He watched as she lifted one hand to tuck a straight strand of dark brown hair behind her ear, then seconds later pull it free once more, then he dragged his attention away to start his presentation. 'Right, I think that's enough from me,' he said eventually. 'Are there any questions I can answer for anyone?'

There was a silence in the room, then someone cleared her throat slightly. 'Catherine Earnshaw from the *Bridby Gazette*,' her voice said clearly. She was looking straight at him now and her face was almost back to her normal colour.

'Yes?'

'What timescale are you looking at for this project? I can't see anything in the folder.'

For a moment they looked at each

other. 'Good question,' he said. 'The construction period I can tell you, that's fifty-four weeks from start to finish. But obviously that's only if the project is approved. If the people of the town give the go-ahead, only then can a start date be set.'

Catherine nodded slightly but said no more. She didn't need to because she'd set the ball rolling and now there were several queries from other members of the audience. He couldn't speak to her again until the whole presentation was over and people were lingering over coffee.

This was his event, an important day in the progress of a project that meant so much to him, even if he hated the presentation process compared with the solo design period and the activity of the construction itself, but as soon as he could, Sean excused himself from a dull conversation and walked over to where Catherine was studying the 3D model of the development.

'So, what do you think of it?'

She glanced up at him. 'Difficult to tell,' she said coolly with the faintest of smiles. He might have been a complete stranger. Ouch.

'Oh?'

'These models are all well and good when they're on display in a room like this, but that's not how the building will be. They don't show the setting, how wide the nearby roads are, how the height of the building would affect the skyline, the effect on neighbouring properties. And so on.'

'That's why the artists' impressions in the folders put the whole building into context,' he said easily. 'And there are computer simulated images to show exactly what you've mentioned. Though there's no substitute for the real thing, hence the site visits we've planned.'

'Well, I'll be interested to see it. So will the people of Bridby. We will naturally be doing a big feature in next week's *Gazette*.'

'So you will interview me after all.'

She almost smiled. Almost. 'No, I

50

won't. I came along today but one of our reporters will be writing the feature.'

'I see. All right, we're honoured to have the editor here for the launch of the project, anyway.'

He saw her bite down on her lip, then she folded her arms across her chest and looked directly at him. 'I wasn't expecting to see you here,' she said evenly.

'Really? Why not?'

'You know why not.'

Sean had to admit he was surprised, first that she'd drawn attention to herself by asking the question during the press conference and now that she didn't flinch from his gaze.

'Didn't Bill tell you this was my project?'

'No,' she said casually with a smile that he somehow knew wasn't genuine. 'I suppose we were talking of other things.'

Well, that put him in his place, Sean thought. Other, more important, things, that was what she'd meant. And for some reason it bothered him that although she had almost admitted that she'd been mistaken about him, she was still trying to provoke him.

He smiled at her. 'I won't keep you. I know you're busy and have so many important things to do. But I do like this image of you.'

'This image?'

'You as an editor. It's a different side to you. Not like the one I know from reading your story.'

'My story?'

Yes, there was that look in her eyes again, the flicker that showed she wasn't quite so composed as she tried to make out.

'Your story, Catherine Earnshaw. How are you described in Wuthering Heights? 'A wild, wicked slip — with the bonniest eye, and sweetest smile, and lightest foot in the parish.' It's all right being the professional editor but don't forget to be that, too.'

He'd wanted a reaction and he got

one. Her eyes widened and the colour flooded her face once more.

And then, because he never chased after any woman and had no intention of doing so now, he flicked one last glance at her face and sauntered away. He walked across the room and fell into conversation with a man he assumed to be from Bridby Council, smiling and nodding as he listened to the stranger without hearing a word he said.

Catherine Discovers More About Sean

It was a view to die for. Catherine looked out over Bridby Bay and told herself for the hundredth time how perfect everything was. She loved every bit of it — the busy harbour with its cluster of red and white pantiled houses hugging the cliff sides, the beach beyond stretching out to the headland and its treacherous rocks, the outline of the abbey ruins against the sky from its position high above the town.

This was the view from her office and it was almost too good to be true. She was in the very heart of it — in more ways than one.

Forcing her attention away from the town she never knew she loved so much until she returned to it, Catherine looked at the men sitting opposite her on one of the new sofas. Their introduction had raised eyebrows in the newsroom, she knew, but she was determined to introduce an informality into the atmosphere of the paper as well as improving communication between the staff. Regular meetings in the editor's office was one way to do that.

'So we'll start advertising next week for a new senior reporter and a trainee,' she said, glancing from one face to the other.

'Two new reporters will make a big difference,' Barrie Amberly, the deputy editor, commented and she could hear the reluctant pleasure in his voice.

'We're going to have more pages to fill. There's so much happening in this town we could publish a newspaper every evening.' She looked at their blank faces and felt her spirits drop. She had to go slowly. 'We could do, but we won't. And we'd better get back to work if we want to do that this week!'

Both men got to their feet with something like relief, Barrie shuffling the papers in his hand and Angus Williams, the news editor, fiddling with his tie. 'It starts to get busy on Tuesdays, er, Cathy ... ' His voice tailed away as it often seemed to do part-way through a sentence.

'Catherine,' she said firmly after the shortest of pauses.

For as long as she could remember she'd hated her name. Her parents had had no idea of the burden they had saddled her with when they'd chosen — accidentally, they claimed — to name her after one of literature's most famous female characters. Someone at university had actually suggested she use an alias in her journalism, but she'd stubbornly refused to change it and determined to make it her own instead. Just as she would make the Gazette her own as well, no matter how long it took.

'Catherine. Right. We'll bring the page proofs in for you read tomorrow when they're ready, if that's what you want.' Angus nodded at Catherine, a pained expression on his face that could almost have been called a smile.

'I do.'

'It's not something Ronnie ever did, but . . . '

'Thanks, Angus, Barrie. Goodnight.' She smiled at them nicely, but firmly and finally they disappeared. Alone at last, she leant back with a deep sigh and closed her eyes.

'Getting you down already?'

Her eyes flew open to see a smiling Helen Padley in the doorway, jacket in hand.

'I'm looking forward to the challenge,' Catherine said carefully and Helen laughed out loud.

'I'm off now, Catherine. The kids will be screaming for something to eat and watching TV instead of doing their homework. See you tomorrow?'

'Sure. Have a good evening, Helen.'

She was lucky, Catherine thought as she watched her friend go. A great job in this gorgeous place. Wandering over to her desk she looked out of the window once more. Outside, late afternoon was turning into early evening and the June sunshine danced across the waters of the bay. That view again. She glanced down at her watch. Not even six yet. There was plenty of daylight left, so she reached out for the phone and punched in a familiar number.

'Dad? It's me. I'm leaving the office, but I think I'll go for a walk before I come home. What time were you wanting to eat? I don't want to be a pain . . .' She listened for several moments. 'That sounds great. I won't be late, I promise.'

She walked around the harbour and she lingered to watch the fishing boats preparing for another night at sea. The activity had fascinated her, as it had at the nearby lifeboat station, where the volunteer crews maintained the boats that had saved so many lives. And suddenly, out of nowhere, came Helen's voice telling her that the architect behind the conference and community centre plan was one of the lifeboat volunteers.

Sean Radford-Jones. What a fool I made of myself with that man, she thought. She halted and gazed out across the beach. It was too early in the season for there to be many visitors and the seafront was almost deserted.

She slipped off her shoes and rolled up the legs of her smart trouser suit before running down the steps and on to the beach.

She walked across the sand, enjoying the feel of the grains between her toes, bending occasionally to sift through the driftwood and pebbles washed up by the tide.

Picking her way carefully through the rocks, she rounded the headland and her eyes immediately rested on the tall, muscular figure of the man she'd been trying not to think about. He was sitting on a large boulder, his blond head bent in concentration as he wrote, or drew, something in a small notebook.

The next moment Sean Radford-Jones looked up and their eyes met. This time he was as surprised to see her as she was to see him, and he blinked once or twice as he gazed at her with those intense blue eyes.

'Hi,' she said. Tongue-tied, like a gauche teenager. How ridiculous.

'Hey there.' Getting to his feet, he closed the notebook with a snap and shoved it into his back pocket. He was dressed casually again, jeans and a heavy sweater over a shirt, but there was no mistaking the type of man he was. Composed, confident and very, very sure of himself. 'It seems we had the same idea.'

'Yes.' Was that all she could say? Words of one syllable?

'Another unexpected meeting.'

'I didn't come down here looking for you if that's what you're thinking . . . '

He folded his arms across his chest and surveyed her. 'That's not what I meant. Don't be so defensive, Catherine.'

He was being honest. He wasn't teasing her for once, because it really was the last place he'd expected to see Catherine Earnshaw.

'What were you doing, when I

disturbed you, I mean.' Her voice was softer now, as if she'd decided that hostility wasn't worth the effort.

'You didn't disturb me. You could say I'm mixing business with pleasure. It's a beautiful evening . . . '

Her gaze swept the bay, taking in the detail of the town as it hugged the shore. 'I love this time of the year. When the days start getting longer and you can feel the air warming up around you ready for summer.'

He seemed to consider her words, then reached into his pocket and brought out the notepad. Flipping it open to the first page, he handed it to her. 'I was seeking inspiration.'

'Do you need inspiration?' she asked curiously. 'You finished the design for your project, I've seen the model and all the plans, remember?'

'Not for that project, no. But the next one.'

Already he was preparing to move on. Catherine looked down at the notepad in her hand and at the image sketched there. In a few strokes, bold and confident ones, she could tell by their very brevity, he had created a startling and compelling image of one of the most famous sights in the town. She turned her gaze to the original, the abbey, standing proud and tall on the southern headland, then back to his sketch.

'You're not designing an abbey, are you?'

'No, unfortunately. I'd like to do that.' He saw her questioning look and smiled properly for the first time. 'Build something that lasts for centuries.'

'But it's a ruin now.'

He shrugged. 'It's still there, in that impossible place. Making the statement it was originally intended to make. When you imagine what they had to work with and yet they created that. For all our modern materials and techniques, what we're doing now is just a pale imitation of what was done back then.'

'I suppose what I do can trace its

roots back to the abbey, too,' she said slowly after a slight pause. 'Monks were the chroniclers of their time, after all. What's a newspaper or a magazine but the same thing on paper instead of parchment? Or even on the internet.'

The lazy smile was back. 'So you're a descendant of the Venerable Bede?'

She laughed at that. 'Not quite. I don't think I'd have fitted in with their way of life, do you?'

'I think you'd have caused havoc in the cloisters.'

'I like the picture,' she said with a sudden shyness.

'Thanks.' He pocketed the book. 'So, if you're not looking for inspiration, why are you here?'

'I've been hunting for treasure.' She opened her hand and showed him three small fragments of rock. 'That's what I used to call it when I was little. Do you know this stone is unique to this coastline?'

Now it was Sean's turn to look out to sea, and he ran a hand through his short blond hair. 'That's what I like about here. It reminds me of where I grew up.'

Intrigued, Catherine looked up at him, aware, as always, that his height made her five foot seven inches seem quite insignificant. 'In Belfast?' she asked curiously and he turned back to face her.

'My parents' house overlooks Belfast Lough. It's like this, the shoreline's full of the unexpected. My brothers and I knew every inch of that shore. We lived out there as kids, whatever the weather.'

A childhood in the open air, watching the tides and the changing seasons. 'You have brothers?'

'I'm the middle one of three.'

She thought about that, and her own family. 'My brother hates the sea. He lives in the desert now.'

'So your dad told me. Dubai.'

She nodded then they lapsed into a silence that was comfortable rather than awkward. 'My feet are cold,' Catherine said eventually because she was beginning to realise that it wasn't the time of year for a barefoot stroll on the beach.

She turned and almost stumbled on a slippery rock but when he reached out a hand to help, she shrugged it away. He didn't comment and they crossed the beach together, then he waited while she brushed away the sand and slipped on her flat shoes.

'Are you walking home?'

She nodded.

'Then I'll go with you part of the way. We pass my place, I might even let you see my house.'

'I heard you were building a house,' she said, then instantly regretted her enthusiasm. She wasn't sure why, but the last thing she wanted was for Sean to know she had been discussing him with someone else.

'Renovating one,' he corrected. 'Come on. I'll show you.'

They set off up the hill.

'You seem determined to write about me in your newspaper,' he commented casually, breaking their companionable silence and forcing her thoughts back to the present. Now he definitely was teasing her and Catherine felt a faint flush on her cheeks that she hoped was merely the effect of the wind blowing in from the sea.

'I'm not sure . . . ' she began but he interrupted her.

'I had a long chat with your friend, Helen, this morning for her feature.'

'It's an important subject,' she said defensively. Just as it was important not to make it personal — about him instead of his design project.

'You don't have to convince me about that.' He paused for a moment and she felt his eyes on her. 'And Carl says I'm to be the first in your series on the lifeboat crew.'

'I didn't know you were with the lifeboat,' she lied for no other reason than to pretend that she hadn't given him a thought when out of his company.

She followed him through the open gates as they arrived on to the site she hadn't been able to see in the dark on that night not so long ago when a delivery truck had blocked her way.

It was fantastic. Despite the rough surroundings during the construction work, there was no doubt the building was both beautiful and impressive. Built in traditional Bridby stone, it was as large as a barn but the rows of windows that stretched across two floors showed it had been used as a dwelling before.

'We've taken down the scaffolding now we've finished the roof,' Sean was saying. 'The major external work's done at last, but there's still enough to do inside, even to make it habitable.'

'It's amazing,' she said slowly. 'It's massive . . . and perfect.'

'You like it,' he said softly, a statement more than a question, and Catherine's gaze was drawn to his face. He was smiling slightly and she found herself responding in kind.

'Who wouldn't like it? And this site, you must have the best views in Bridby!'

'Yeah, I'll show you inside.' He

unlocked the front door and led the way into the interior. He was right, there was a lot of work to do, but she was fascinated as he led her from room to room, explaining his plans for the sort of place most people could only dream of.

'I suppose you should expect an architect to design himself a stunning home,' she said with a disingenuous smile, and he forced his mind to concentrate.

'I've wanted to do this as long as I can remember.' *And I've wanted to kiss you almost as long*, he thought.

'I can understand that.' She turned and led the way downstairs and into the sunlight. 'When will it be finished?'

He laughed and glanced at the messy site around him. 'That's the question! Right now, it feels like never.'

'Surely you have a schedule of works?'

Trust Catherine to cut to the chase. As organised as he was in his work, somehow he couldn't commit himself to any kind of structured plan when it came to his own house. It was like the rest of his life, he wanted to go with the flow, see where the moment took him.

'Kind of . . . ' he said slowly. 'But what I get done depends on my workload. Right now, I don't have the time to do what I want. Let's just say progress has been slow this winter.'

'You're doing the work yourself?'

She was asking him lots of questions again, but he didn't mind. He liked it that she was interested and the way her forehead wrinkled and she tilted her head as she waited for his answers.

'As much as I can.' He saw her confusion. 'I travelled after university and spent almost a year in Spain working on construction sites. If you want to design good buildings, you have to understand the techniques needed to create them. I've always wanted to do this, it's one of my reasons for being here.'

She nodded but stayed silent and suddenly he had a question of his own. 'What's your reason? What made you give up your life in London to come back here?'

They were standing facing each other in what would one day be his garden and he watched as she blinked and looked away.

'To be with my dad and to take the job at the Gazette.'

He knew a half-truth when he heard one but worryingly he wanted to believe it.

Suddenly aware of the danger, he smiled. 'I can see you'd want to be with Bill, but the Gazette? There must have been another reason. What would make a top magazine editor travel all those miles to work on a weekly newspaper? Let me guess — broken heart?'

Catherine hesitated. He was smart and he saw things as they were.

'Why does it always have to be a man?' she asked wearily. 'Why can't a woman want something more in life than that? Maybe I wanted what you did, life in a small town where getting up in a morning is a pleasure not a chore.'

He acknowledged that with an almost imperceptible nod of the head. When he lifted a hand to tuck a stray strand of her hair behind one ear, her breath caught in her throat.

For a moment they simply stared at each other and when he spoke his voice was so soft she could barely hear him. 'I don't know what I want from life, but I know what I want to do right now.'

With that he lowered his head and rested his lips on hers in the gentlest kiss she'd ever experienced.

The first noise she heard was a diesel engine, followed by a bleeping sound as if a vehicle were in reverse. Then there was a male voice shouting from somewhere in the distance, away from a world in which being kissed by Sean was the only thing that mattered.

Abruptly he tore his lips from hers and raised his head, glancing at the watch on his wrist. 'A delivery,' he said tersely in a voice that wasn't quite so even or assured as normal. 'They can only do it when I'm around. I forgot.'

She'd forgotten everything, Catherine thought, trying to marshal thoughts that had been scattered to the four winds. Never had she known such a gentle kiss, such a passionate kiss . . .

She watched as he strode over to the truck and directed the driver to where he wanted the delivery set down. Then he walked back towards her, seemingly unconcerned and unaffected by the kiss they'd just shared, whereas she was shattered.

'Underfloor heating,' he said by way of explanation and Catherine remembered why she was there in the first place. To see his house.

'I have to go.' He raised his eyebrows in enquiry and she felt herself blush under his gaze. 'Dad's preparing dinner and — and I have work to do.'

'Work. Right.' He was smiling at her.

Resolutely, she did not look back, but her mind was in overdrive. It was just a kiss, her brain told her heart. It didn't mean anything — it was just a kiss.

But ten minutes later when she unlatched the gate of Holly Cottage her heart was still having none of it.

Catherine lifted out her briefcase and closed the car door. It was one of the idiosyncrasies of the Gazette that staff had to leave their cars in a public car park which could be problem in the busy summer months, she thought with a smile. Just as well she usually walked to work.

'Half day?'

Startled, she swung around and found herself looking into a pair of blue eyes and a tanned face. Eyes that held something new behind the usual teasing gleam — hostility and resentment. It was the first time she'd seen Sean since her visit to his home and that kiss — and she wasn't sure how to react.

'Sorry?'

'It's midday. Not your normal start time, I'm sure.'

She couldn't help but remember the gentle sensation of his kiss but there was no doubting the unfriendliness in Sean's manner now and her chin rose in defiance. 'I've been at a board meeting in York.' The last thing she'd wanted to do after a late night at the printing works, but new editors didn't have any choice.

'I've seen the Gazette,' Sean said, lifting up a copy of the latest newspaper, published only that morning. She noticed that he was also carrying a cardboard tube of designs so he was likely on his way to or from a meeting, too. She knew he parked his car here, because she'd seen him once or twice from her office window, though she'd never mentioned it to anyone.

'Oh.'

'Nice feature. Your friend did a great job. Shame about the Editor's comment on page five, though.' He flipped open the paper and began to read. ' 'The conference centre is undoubtedly a clever and striking design. The people of Bridby have to decide for themselves if a new building on such a scale is what they want — and what the town needs. Many other towns have conference centres that have proved very successful but not many towns have the other attractions, natural beauties and sense of community that this one does'.'

She said nothing.

He closed the paper. 'If you want to get back at me, Catherine, don't do it through my work.'

That shocked her. 'Get back at you?'

'What did you call it? A good laugh at your expense? I never thought you'd do this. I never thought you'd attack the project to get your revenge on me.' He shook his head in resignation but his eyes still betrayed his resentment.

'Now just hold on a minute.' She was starting to get angry. She'd written those words, she'd agonised over them, actually — and she stood by every one. 'I did not attack your project. And as for 'getting back at you' . . . .Don't be absurd. I was asking the question — does the town want the project. That's my job — to ask questions.'

'Leading questions? Oh, you have all the answers, don't you, Catherine?

Especially to the questions nobody else wants to ask.'

She felt the sting of hurt, but also of her own deep resentment. She'd taken great care with the feature and the editorial, and now here was this man, dismissing her efforts . . .

Then the penny dropped. Suddenly she understood why he was so resentful of her mild and uncontroversial editorial.

'I get it,' she said, trying to swallow the pain at the realisation of exactly why he'd kissed her on that magical evening.

It shouldn't cause her pain anyway, she told herself furiously. It wasn't worth it. 'So that's what the little charm offensive the other day was all about. I should have known. Special treatment, is that what you were hoping for? Well, sorry to disappoint you, but that's not how I work.'

His eyes narrowed and for a moment she thought she saw a flicker of warmth, maybe at the memory of their kiss, but the next moment it was gone. 'Not special treatment,' he ground out through gritted teeth. 'I expected you to be fair, that's all.'

'I was fair. It's not up to me or my newspaper to put out press releases for your project. We put down the facts and invite people to make up their own minds. If that's not enough for you, then tough!'

She saw him bite down on his lip as if he were trying to control a temper she hadn't known existed. 'People look to you,' he said slowly. 'This is the best thing to happen in this town for years. It's not only about a new facility — it will mean jobs, real jobs, for local people who otherwise would have to leave the town. So it's not as photo-genic as an eleventh-century abbey but it will make a real difference to people's lives which has to be more important than preserving the past for the past's sake.'

He turned to go, then hesitated for a moment. 'As for the charm offensive

. . . You do yourself an injustice, Catherine. I didn't kiss you to win favours for my project. And I don't think you kissed me back to trash it either. Think about it.'

She refused to watch him walk away. Instead she took her briefcase and headed for the Gazette offices.

She was used to confrontation — she'd spent her working life in a profession that demanded toughness and a strong sense of self-belief, but for some reason Sean Radford-Jones's disapproval had hurt. Really hurt.

⋆　⋆　⋆

The first thing she saw when she walked into the editorial department was a huge bouquet of flowers sitting on Helen Padley's desk.

Her friend was surrounded by eager colleagues and, ignoring her own thoughts, Catherine dutifully stepped over to admire the blooms.

'Aren't these gorgeous, Catherine?'

Helen asked with the widest of smiles.

'They're lovely. Your husband has good taste.'

They were gorgeous — lilies and freesias in a deep purple, flowers that Catherine liked better than any others on earth.

'They're not from Dave,' Helen said with a grin. 'They're from Sean Radford-Jones!'

For one horror-struck moment Catherine thought he was having an affair with her friend, but fortunately Helen hadn't finished speaking. 'They're a thank you for the feature. I told him I was really nervous about doing it. I mean, it's so important — and he's sent me these to say thank you and that he liked it.'

'It was a good feature,' Catherine said automatically, then she turned and walked into her office, closing the door behind her. She sat down at the desk, tears pricking her eyes, but she resolutely blinked them away. She would not cry over Sean Radford-Jones. She would not.

Fool, she told herself harshly. You're not the heroine in a book and there's no such thing as a hero. It was just a kiss. That's all. It didn't mean anything. He has his job to do and you have yours.

* * *

Sean walked into his own office to be met by the smiling face of his office manager. Bernice had started out as his receptionist, but he'd quickly changed her job title and almost doubled her salary because of the efficiency and cheerfulness with which she ran his business. Which was great normally but 'cheerful' was probably the last thing he needed right now.

'Good morning! How did the meeting go?' she asked brightly.

'So-so.' He rested the tube of designs on her desk and looked down at what she was reading. The Gazette. He might have known.

'Have you seen the Gazette?' Bernice

asked, excitedly. She was a motherly woman in her late fifties who had lived in Bridby all her life and couldn't be more proud of the town and its attractions. 'It's a lovely feature. Colour drawings and everything.'

'Did you see the editorial on page five?' he asked abruptly.

'Oh yes, but the Editor has to stay impartial,' she said knowingly. 'My Brian used to teach Catherine Earnshaw at the high school.'

'Yeah?'

'She's done very well for herself, has Catherine, and now she's back home to sort out the Gazette.'

He smiled but said nothing as he headed for the sanctuary of his office. Once he was behind his own desk he opened the newspaper and read her words again.

All right, she had to remain impartial but the least she could have done was to warn him. A phone call, a note.

He should have known she would argue with him. She'd defended her actions calmly and logically and that had made him even more angry.

Tossing the newspaper to one side, he pressed a button on the intercom. 'Bernice? I think we should get two dozen copies of the Gazette. Can you get them, or send Colin when he gets back from the timber supplier?'

Ending the message, he sat back in his chair. He could hear Catherine's voice as she stood up to him. *You wanted special treatment, well, that's not how I work. Sorry to disappoint you.*

Sometime soon he'd hold her to account. Sooner or later, she'd acknowledge the scorching attraction between them, and the nagging ache that never seemed to leave him would be eased.

Whatever she might say, whatever she might do, Catherine Earnshaw knew just as well as he that the kiss had only been the beginning.

'You Should Go With Sean'

'How's business this weather?' Sean Radford-Jones asked as he stood at the garage.

Dave Padley grinned and shrugged as he handed over a set of car keys to him. 'Not bad,' he said. 'It will get better in the summer. It needs to, with three kids spending every penny I earn — and more.'

Sean smiled. His lifeboat colleague was the epitome of the happily married man, whatever his vocal objections and it suited him, though it wasn't the kind of lifestyle he'd ever been tempted to embark on himself. He couldn't see the attraction — he liked women, just as he liked visiting new places and sampling different foods, but a lifelong commitment? Not his thing . . . Shaking his head slightly, he grinned at the other man. 'So you're looking forward to the summer season?'

'Except we'll be busier than ever on the lifeboat.'

He nodded. Sean, who had been brought up by the water knew well enough that the better weather brought increased risks. In the summer, more people were lured into danger by the seeming serenity of the sea, which hid its dangers well below the surface until it was often too late.

'Hello, you two!'

A sound in the doorway of the garage disturbed them, and both men turned. Helen Padley was standing there, dressed for her role as Bridby Gazette features writer, and wearing the brightest smile Sean had seen all week.

Dave glanced at his watch. 'You're finished early.'

'Time off for good behaviour.' Helen walked up to her husband and pecked him on the cheek, before she turned back to Sean. 'Thank you for the gorgeous flowers.'

'You're welcome,' he said easily. 'I just wanted to say thanks, what you wrote was excellent. Really, it was terrific.' He'd sent her the bouquet on impulse and he couldn't really say why except that anyone so worried about doing a good job needed to know she'd done a great job.

'Hmm, that's all right, but I'm not sure about those flowers,' Dave muttered with a grin that showed he wasn't quite serious. 'She'll expect them every week and I'll have to foot that bill.'

'Well, I deserve them. I'm having a good day. Guess what? Catherine wants me to work an extra day each week!' Helen said excitedly. 'She says any day is fine and I can work my hours around school, or work from home whenever I want.'

'You're being appreciated at last,' Dave commented with a smile that showed how proud he was of his wife.

He had good reason, Sean thought. Helen had been very nervous during their interview, but the end result had been superb. He wondered why she'd lacked so much confidence about her work.

'I know. About time, isn't it? It's fantastic now Catherine's taken over. There's a really good atmosphere in the office now — it's only those silly old men who are giving her such a bad time.'

Sean listened but said nothing. It's only those silly old men giving Catherine such a bad time . . .

'They're idiots. They don't like having a female boss,' Dave commented and his wife laughed, slipping an arm through his in a gesture of affection.

'As if you wouldn't be the same if it happened to you!'

Sean tossed the car keys in his hand and decided it was time to go. Dave Padley had been his colleague in the lifeboat crew for almost a year and now he was getting to know Helen, too, he was pleased things were going well for her. 'Thanks, Dave. It's made a big difference getting the starter motor fixed today,' he said, making a move towards the door, but her voice halted him.

'You are coming to the dinner, aren't you?' Helen asked, changing the subject to the forthcoming annual lifeboat fundraising event.

The dinner. He'd almost forgotten it, though it was such an important event for everyone connected with the rescue charity, held at a top-class hotel just outside the town. 'Maybe.'

'You have to come,' she protested. 'It's our year for organising and everything has to be perfect!'

'I'm flattered that you need me to make it perfect,' he said laughing. 'Of course I'll be there. I know how much it matters to the lifeboat station.'

'Good. So who are you bringing with you?'

Who would be his date? He shrugged. 'I've no idea.'

'Too much choice? Too many eager women waiting for the call?' Helen asked good-naturedly and he smiled dutifully.

'I'll let you know if I find someone.'

'If you find someone? Pull the other one!'

'Bye, Dave, Helen.' Refusing to be drawn any further, he walked towards the door, but when he emerged into the bright spring sunshine he paused for a moment.

She was right. He wouldn't have a problem finding a date for the dinner, even at only a few days' notice. There was Lorna in the council's finance department, or Jane, whose brother was a crewman on the lifeboat's other watch. Then there was Ellie, who ran the Smugglers' Inn. Yes, there was any number of women he could ask.

Maybe he would. Then again, maybe he wouldn't because he had some unfinished business, which was distracting him from everything else. A woman who would speak her mind on any subject, but blushed when a man looked at her, and who seemed cool, calm and collected until a kiss revealed the passionate nature underneath that layer of ice . . .

He couldn't even think of any other woman until this one was out of his system.

★   ★   ★

Catherine had spent the week concentrating on her job. There was so much to do and now she was beginning to understand how the Gazette worked, she could start to implement some changes. It would be easier, of course, to work at her desk, but she'd sworn to herself when she'd moved back to Bridby that she wouldn't lock herself away in the office every evening.

That part of her life was over and she wanted this new chapter to be different. So here she was, sample pages and proofs spread out across the dining table and on a quiet evening like this alone at the cottage it didn't seem like work at all.

Somewhere in the distance she heard the sound of a car, but it was only when she heard the sound of someone opening the front door that she glanced up at the clock on the mantelpiece. It was after 8.30 already — she really hadn't noticed the time and her dad was home already. With company.

She recognised his voice immediately. She hadn't seen Sean Radford-Jones since the day they'd argued in the car park. She'd been at the printers on Thursday night when he visited for his regular chess game with Bill Earnshaw, which had suited her perfectly.

Of course she knew they'd have to meet eventually but every extra day she had to compose herself helped. It helped to erase the memory of that exquisite kiss, and the memory, too, of how her foolish daydreams had been shattered when she found out the truth behind it and he'd questioned her professionalism . . .

But that was all in the past and she was resolved to be polite and distant towards him from now on.

'Dad!' She looked up as they entered the room. 'I was going to come and pick you up. You said you'd call.'

'Hello, love. I forgot my phone, and when I saw Sean outside the hall he said he'd give me a lift,' her father said cheerily.

He was a man of medium height but he looked small and insignificant alongside the tall form of Sean Radford-Jones, who was dressed almost exactly as he had been the last time they'd met in this room.

She acknowledged him with a brief nod and in return he smiled. 'Hey, Catherine,' he said easily as if there had never been anything between them, let alone a passionate kiss and a bitter argument.

'What's the point of having a phone if you always forget to take it with you, Dad,' she complained mildly as she resolutely turned her attention back to her father.

'I know, I know,' Bill said with a grin

at his friend. 'I'm too old to learn new things, like those phones.'

'You're learning things on your course,' she pointed out, but he merely shrugged and moved to stand behind her chair. 'And then there's tonight's history lecture.'

'What are you up to, Katie? Not working again?'

She knew without looking at him that Sean had walked over to stand beside her father. 'Just some planning. I'm working on designs for the newspaper. It's long overdue a new look.'

Bill Earnshaw patted his daughter's shoulder. 'They're very good, aren't they, Sean?'

Sean let his eyes drift over the papers spread almost the length of the table. He had to admit to himself that part of the attraction for giving Bill a lift home was the opportunity to see Catherine again.

'You're planning to use a large picture on the front page,' he commented. 'I like it. It's more effective than filling it with words.'

'Well, words are my business, but you're right. And we are lucky enough to have a fantastically photogenic town and a very talented young photographer, so we're going to make the most of them — until Neil's snapped up by a daily newspaper or a magazine, that is.'

Catherine started to gather the pages from the table but he made no move to either help or step to one side so she could get up from her chair.

'You're sacrificing your words for an image?'

She looked up at him, pages in hand. 'Not sacrificing. It's the juxtaposition of the two that matters. If we filled the Gazette with pretty photos people would only flick through it for about ten seconds. If we have columns of boring black and white text, no-one will ever buy it.'

He nodded. It was something he understood. 'Good design isn't just about aesthetics. It's no use something being beautiful if it's not practical.'

'You're talking about buildings?' she asked curiously.

He thrust his hands into his pockets. 'Sure. What would be the point of a public building if the entrances are inaccessible, or an art gallery where bad lighting makes it impossible to see the paintings? On the other hand, what would life be without something good to look at?'

For a moment she looked at him, then she seemed to remember where she was and shook her head slightly as if trying to banish an unwelcome thought from her mind. 'I should clear up,' she said. He obligingly moved to one side at last and watched as she packed the proofs away in her briefcase, closing the lid with a defiant snap.

'You caught me on the hop, Dad,' she said with a vague smile and a nod in the direction of the kitchen.

'It smells good, love.'

'It's lasagne.'

'Smashing! Are you going to stay, Sean?' Bill Earnshaw said suddenly, before turning to his daughter. 'We've got plenty, haven't we, Katie?'

An invitation to dinner. Now that idea interested him but he knew someone who would think differently . . . 'I'd love to, Bill, but I'm sure your meal was planned for two only,' he began, but to his surprise Catherine interrupted him.

'It's no problem. You're very welcome to stay. It won't be long.'

Her voice was cool, her expression bland and inscrutable. With a face bare of make-up and wearing old clothes that were probably relics from her teenage years, she certainly wasn't dressing to impress. But then again, she hadn't been expecting him, he consoled himself, and although he knew she'd only seconded the invitation to please her father, it was a start.

★   ★   ★

Transferring portions of pasta on to three plates, Catherine told herself she'd done the right thing. It was the perfect opportunity, she thought, to show Sean Radford-Jones how little he affected her. That he was merely an acquaintance to whom she'd be polite and pleasant when he visited her home as a friend of her father's. It was simple and if she concentrated it would be easy, too. If she didn't let him embarrass or annoy her. Or make her feel like a teenager on her first date.

When she carried the tray through he took it from her and set it down on the table. As she served up their salad and the bread she'd warmed in the oven, Sean insisted on removing the bottle of wine and corkscrew from her father's hands, before opening it in one swift and easy movement.

It was a disconcertingly domestic scene. Three people seated around the dining table, sharing a simple meal and a plain bottle of wine while talking quietly as they ate and drank. Like any three people who knew and liked each other might do.

In the soft light — someone must have turned on the corner lamps, just as she liked — she watched her father as he chatted to his friend. She knew how lonely he'd been since her mother's death, but she had been too far away to do much about it. He'd told her it was OK for her to accept the six-month secondment in the States just weeks later, but it hadn't been OK. She could see that now. He'd been here alone and the weekly phone calls hadn't been enough. Not that he'd ever told her so . . .

He'd been through so much and she wanted him to be happy — nobody deserved that more than her dad — so she was glad she'd asked Sean Radford-Jones to stay for supper. Whatever she thought of him, her father obviously enjoyed his company and that was all that mattered.

It was no surprise her dad liked him. He was good company. What he said was interesting, but he didn't dominate the conversation, listening attentively to others with an occasional comment or question at exactly the right moment. There wasn't harsh line in his profile, she thought as he smiled slightly at something her father said. She had never seen anything so good to look at as the man behind those casual words.

'This is very good,' he said, turning to her suddenly and gesturing towards the food with his fork.

Caught in the act of staring she said the first thing that came into her head. 'Is it?' Stunning repartee. Very impressive, Catherine Earnshaw.

'Katie's a dab hand in the kitchen, even though she's so busy at the newspaper.'

'All that and she cooks as well.'

'Oh yes, I'm a regular Superwoman,' she commented dryly, thinking that however old you were, parents still had the capacity to embarrass you in front of people.

'You know how to make all these fancy things!' her dad said proudly and Catherine groaned inwardly.

'Lasagne's not fancy. You had it in

Italy. I knew you liked it when we were there.' She looked at Sean. 'Dad and I went to Venice and Verona last summer.'

'I know. I've seen the photographs.'

It wasn't easy, pretending indifference, when he could make the simplest words sound so seductive and enticing. And if that didn't put her at enough of a disadvantage, it made her even more uncomfortable to imagine him looking at her picture when she didn't even know he existed. She swallowed nervously and set down her own knife and fork on her empty plate.

'I'll clear these . . . ' she began but was interrupted by her father.

'No, you won't,' Bill said firmly as he got to his feet. 'I'll do it. Both you and Sean have been working all day. Let me do it.'

Catherine watched him go in silence, knowing that Sean would say something now they were alone. He didn't disappoint her.

'You don't know how to take a compliment,' he said as he leant over to top up her glass with wine. 'I told you before — you do yourself an injustice. And I'm not talking about your professional reputation here.'

Gazing at the ruby red liquid, Catherine thought about the last time he'd said that phrase to her. That day in the car park.

'Helen liked the flowers you sent her.' She could have bitten out her tongue but it was too late — the words had been said and there was a flicker of interest in his eyes.

'I liked her article.' His voice was deceptively casual but she wasn't fooled for a moment.

'Of course you did. It was a very good article. But . . .'

'But?'

'Well . . .' What could she say? 'You didn't need to send her flowers. They were beautiful, but there was no need. Helen did a fantastic feature but that's her job. You wouldn't expect a present for doing your job — and neither does a journalist.'

'What's the matter, Catherine?' he said eventually. 'Is it the flowers you didn't like, or the fact that I didn't send them to you?'

'Oh, for heaven's sake!'

'Don't be embarrassed about being jealous. If it's flowers you want, I can easily fix that.'

His voice was low and teasing and Catherine felt the heat rising inside her. Her whole body seemed to respond to his words, to the sound of his voice, to his very presence . . .

'I'm talking seriously here. About whether it is appropriate for someone in your position — an architect and a developer, I mean — to send a gift to someone who needs to maintain an independent and unbiased view.'

'Ah, so we get back to the crux of the problem,' he commented with an irritating calm, as he leant back in his chair and folding his arms across his chest.

'Which is?'

'You never liked the project in the first place.'

'That isn't true.'

'I remember what you said at the presentation.'

'You're misinterpreting what I said that day, in fact . . . '

At the sound of a door opening they both looked up. 'Uh-oh. Are you two arguing?' Bill Earnshaw asked as he returned to the room and retook his seat at the table.

'We're having a discussion. Catherine thinks my nasty development will spoil the unique beauty of her home town and doesn't want to hear differently.'

This was easier to deal with than flirting. She could forget how attracted she was to him when she was reminded how irritating he really was. 'Whereas Sean takes the view that it's progress at all costs,' she said with a smile at her father. 'So you see it's not an argument, just a healthy debate. What do you think, Dad?'

He shook his head and laughed softly. 'Oh no! Don't ask me. People my age don't have an opinion. According to those who make the decisions, anyway.'

'Dad!' she protested. 'You know that's not true.'

'Isn't it? How many retired ladies did you feature in your women's magazine, Katie? I don't think I saw a single one in all the years you were the editor.'

She stared at him. 'Well, I suppose, but that age group wasn't in our demographics,' she began.

'Ah, demographics,' a soft voice said to her left and she threw Sean a dirty look. It seemed everyone wanted to provoke her tonight.

'Our target market wasn't that age group. And it's not as if there aren't magazines for older people. You buy them yourself!' She thought for a moment, then asked suspiciously, 'Are there some women on your local history course? You're getting some very feminist ideas all of a sudden, Dad.'

'I was talking about it with a very nice lady called Mary, but I can come up with my own ideas, Katie,' he said patiently as if talking to a child.

'Demographics! We never had demographics in my day.'

Now she was amused. 'Yes you did. What did you have in the shop, anything you felt like stocking whether it sold or not? No way. You stocked what your customers wanted to buy. You knew your customers' profile, even if you didn't call it 'demographics'.'

'I think we should quit while we're ahead, Bill,' Sean said with a conspiratorial half-smile at his friend. He'd obviously enjoyed their exchange and had no qualms about showing it. 'Or at least while we're still in one piece.'

Her father chuckled. 'Katie's never lost for words. Her mother used to say she was so sharp she would cut herself.'

'She sure likes to speak her mind.'

'Would you mind not talking about me as if I'm not here?' They both looked across at her in fake innocence. 'I know what you're doing. It's a typical male trick and I'm not falling for it. So let's change the subject. Any suggestions?'

Sean raised his glass to her in mock salute. 'All right. Let me say how much I've enjoyed dinner. I'd like to return the favour, in my humble caravan, no less — but not next week. I'm on call for the lifeboat from Friday.'

'That's bad timing. It's the fundraising dinner on Saturday — and you're on call,' Bill exclaimed.

'Hopefully we won't have to go out. But somebody has to be on call, even at the dinner. Are you going?'

'Yes, I am. Dad's coming with me.'

She felt rather than heard her father's sigh. 'Oh Katie, I've told you. It's not really my kind of do. You should be going out with a young man, not your old dad.'

'You're not old,' she said with an encouraging smile. 'Anyway, it will be a nice evening.'

'All that rich food. You know I don't like it.' It was like a bad soap opera — Catherine knew exactly what was coming next and she was powerless to stop it. Just as she was powerless to stop

105

the blood rushing to her cheeks when he finally said the words. 'You should go with Sean.'

'Dad!' she murmured through gritted teeth. 'Don't say that. Sean might have plans already. You can't just expect him to . . .'

It was perfect, Sean thought. He hadn't even thought about taking Catherine to the dinner because he knew she would never accept his offer of a date. But this was perfect.

'Actually, I don't have plans and it would an honour to take you to the dinner, Catherine.' She didn't miss his deliberate emphasis on the word 'honour' and he allowed himself a small smile as he sat back in satisfaction and waited for her to try to wriggle out of it.

'I really don't think . . .'

'Go on, love. You'll have a much better time with Sean than you will with me.'

Could it be any more embarrassing? Her dad fixing her up with an escort. 'I'm not going there to enjoy myself.

I'm going because the Gazette's sponsoring the event,' she protested, knowing she was losing the argument.

'But you will enjoy it if you go with someone your own age, Katie.'

She looked at him in exasperation. The last thing she wanted to do was hurt her father's feelings. He thought he was being kind, offering to stand down in Sean's favour, and there was no way she could tell him why it was the worse thing he could have done. 'All right,' she said with bad grace. 'I'll go with you.'

'Don't bother to thank me,' Sean said with a gleam in his eye that did nothing to ease her misgivings, though it did make her slightly ashamed of her bad manners. And she shouldn't let her dad know how she felt — both about his friend and the thought of spending a whole evening in his company.

But the object of her rudeness didn't seem to mind. 'Right!' He got to his feet and held out his hand to her father. 'Night, Bill. See you Thursday.'

'Goodnight, Sean. Thank you for the lift.'

'You're welcome. Thank you for dinner.'

Catherine hesitated, then followed him into the hall. A private conversation with Sean was generally a bad idea because he always made it personal, but somehow she couldn't resist.

'Making sure I leave the premises?' He was grinning at her as he grabbed a rather battered waxed jacket from the coat hook, slinging it over one shoulder with his customary ease and confidence.

'Do I have to?' she countered and his brow quirked.

'You needn't look so forlorn,' he commented. 'I'm not quite a monster. You'll discover that I'm actually a good date. At least that's what I've been told.'

'Let's get this straight. This isn't a date,' she said stubbornly.

'Isn't it? What are you so afraid of?'

She tried to ignore the fact that he was standing in front of her. 'I'm not afraid of anything.'

'Yes, you are. You can't hide it from me. I know you.'

He was standing there in her home, so sure of himself and in control of everything he said and did.

'You know nothing about me,' she said eventually but he merely smiled.

His voice dropped to almost a whisper. 'Yes, I do, Cathy. I know you cried for a week when your cat died. I know you have a scar on your leg from the time you fell off a pony when you were eleven and how you got back on straightaway. I know you wrote stories sitting on your window seat, stories you wouldn't let anybody read. I know lots about you.'

She opened her mouth to tell him that her name was Catherine, but nothing came out. She wanted to say that she hated being called Cathy, that she wasn't the heroine of a Victorian novel, that she wasn't looking for a romantic hero of her own, that she knew such things didn't exist anyway.

She wanted to tell him all those things, but there was something about the way he said the nickname that stopped her. It didn't sound abrupt or annoying or foolish. It sounded . . . special.

But still. She drew in a deep breath. 'Those are all things from the past,' she said carefully but firmly. 'They're nothing to do with who I am now.'

'Are you sure?' His eyes roamed her face, lingering on her lips, and for one moment she thought he would kiss her. 'I don't think you're so very different from that wild, untamed girl, Cathy.'

She could have argued with him, but she was too busy remembering those days when everything was so simple, when there had been so many possibilities and life was out there for the taking. In those few, soft words he had cut across the years to the girl who really was afraid of nothing and couldn't wait to sample everything life had to offer.

The next time he spoke, however, his voice was brisk and he brought her back to the present with a start.

'If I don't see you before Saturday, I'll pick up you at seven.' He moved towards the door, hesitated for a second, then looked back. 'Just one more thing. Wear something nice.'

And with that he was gone, leaving her speechless and not for the first time feeling completely out of her depth.

A Chance To Become Friends

Catherine smoothed the dress down over her hips and studied herself in the mirror. This was her first social appearance as editor of the Bridby Gazette and it was important that it went well. The key to that, of course, was feeling confident and at ease — which was where the dress came in.

And it wouldn't do any harm to look her best for her 'date' with Sean Radford-Jones.

The word was definitely in inverted commas in her mind. Her father had meant well when he'd suggested Sean take his own place as Catherine's escort, but it had put her in an embarrassing position. That her dad needed to fix her up with a date was bad enough, but that it should be Sean . . .

She had to go to the dinner because it was her job to do so — even if it meant she had to spend the evening with a man who disturbed her in a way she'd never even imagined anyone could disturb her. It wasn't just the way he looked, it was the way he looked at her, what he said, how he said it, the way he provoked her, challenged her, made her feel alive.

But that was something she couldn't tell anyone. Especially Helen Padley.

'I hear you have a hot date for Saturday,' her childhood friend had said, obviously ready for a gossip as she settled herself on the office sofa with a cup of coffee in hand.

Catherine winced, but she hoped that on the outside she looked cool and entirely unconcerned. 'Good grief, Helen,' she said with false unconcern. 'It's not a date. We're just going to the same place, that's all.'

'Going to the same place together. To a dinner. Dressed up. Sounds like a date to me.'

'Helen . . .'

'Hmm. I thought Sean was very coy about who his date was going to be. You're both being very cool about all this.'

'I'm not his date,' Catherine said wearily. She hesitated for a moment. 'It's really embarrassing. My dad suggested it. I felt like a fourteen-year-old whose parents had to arrange for someone to talk to her at a party.'

The other woman giggled. 'Is he matchmaking?'

'Of course not. He knows we don't get on. He just didn't want to go to the dinner and felt sorry for me because of my lack of a social life.'

'Oh, Catherine! You're going out with the best-looking man in Bridby and you make it sound like a punishment. How can you not get on with Sean?'

Yes, how could she not 'get on' with Sean?

This is absurd, she told her reflection. I should be thinking about representing the Gazette, and making a speech, instead of worrying about some man. It wasn't as if they'd even be alone together.

In fact, they'd probably barely speak to one another because she was going to work and he would be surrounded by people he knew. Anyway she was 34 years old and long past the stage of being nervous or ill at ease over a man.

Coming out of her reverie, she could hear voices downstairs. So he was here. Well, there was no getting out of it now, so she grabbed her evening bag — a tiny scrap of beaded silk that could barely take her phone and purse then headed for the stairs.

When she stepped into the kitchen, both men stopped talking and turned to face her, taking in every detail of her appearance.

Sean Radford-Jones didn't need to delude himself about his attractiveness. Evening suits must have been designed with him in mind, she thought hazily.

His six foot two frame filled the suit perfectly and his face was tanned against the white of his shirt. The best-looking man in Bridby, Helen had called him, and he was.

'Here she is!' her father was saying brightly as if Sean hadn't noticed.

Hadn't noticed? He hadn't stirred or moved a muscle yet Catherine knew he'd taken in every inch of her own appearance — the high heels, the silvery grey 1920s-style dress, the shoulders whose white smoothness was only interrupted by two very narrow straps. Suddenly the dress definitely wasn't enough. Long enough or high enough or thick enough, that was.

'Hello, Catherine,' he said.

'You look very nice, love. You're not going to be cold, though, are you?' Bill asked worriedly. 'There's a nip in the air still in the evenings.'

Sean stirred then. With one easy movement he pulled a set of car keys from his pocket, reminding her that indeed they would be alone, on the journey to and from the hotel at least.

'The dress looks perfect from where I'm standing,' he said and for the first time he smiled. 'Don't worry, Bill. I'll take care of her. I'll make sure Catherine's home by midnight.'

Sean gestured that she lead the way which she did, intensely aware that he was following her and watching her every move.

'Did you know you were in Katie's magazine, Sean?' she heard her father say chattily. 'She's been looking you up on the internet and there you were in her magazine!'

'Was I now?'

Thanks, Dad. Thanks for giving him the wrong idea and helping to stoke that aforementioned ego. 'It was just a passing reference,' she said dismissively. 'An interior designer said she liked one of your buildings.'

'Which one?' He sounded amused.

'I don't remember.'

'We've got the page you printed off the computer, Katie.'

'No need, Dad. See you later.' Ignoring the man standing beside her she reached out to kiss her father on the cheek then set off down the path alone.

She had to wait for him by his car while he said goodbye to her father. The weather was beautiful and she didn't need the light shawl she'd picked up at the last minute.

It was an evening that was too good to waste in a busy, hot hotel. It was the sort of evening more suited for a stroll along the beach and she wished that was what they were doing instead . . .

'Sorry,' Sean said with an unrepentant grin before unlocking the door with the remote and holding it open for her. The car was a 4×4, which was entirely practical for a busy architect but not so practical for a woman in a dress.

'You look fantastic, by the way,' he said as he put the car in gear and drove away. 'Nice to see you relaxed for a change.'

She slammed her handbag down on her lap.

'Here we go!' she said in a tone of exasperation, staring out of the window to avoid his intense gaze. 'You never let up, do you?'

'In what way?' He wasn't chastened

at all, in fact his voice was filled with amusement at her display of pique.

'You know.'

He smiled as he watched the road. 'I'm only trying to get you in the mood. You said you didn't want to have a good time so I'm trying to make you as miserable as possible.'

'You sound like you're expecting to enjoy yourself.'

'I already am.'

She did not reply and he was silent for a moment. When he next spoke, his tone was softer and more conciliatory. 'Hey, I'm sorry. That was uncalled for.'

She sighed. This was ridiculous. They were adults and it wasn't Sean's fault that going on a date-that-wasn't-a-date with him was doing all sorts of dangerous things to her peace of mind.

The problem was being alone with him, she told herself. It would be all right when they were at the hotel, among other people where she wouldn't be distracted by those compelling eyes and that voice.

'Forget it.'

'You do look beautiful — but then, I thought you looked beautiful when you'd got your old pyjamas on.'

He wasn't doing anything to help her equilibrium. He seemed determined to flirt with her tonight and she didn't really understand why. Habit? A challenge?

A genuine attraction to her, however fleeting it might be? 'Thank you.'

'Is that the best you can do? Why don't you like compliments, Catherine? I don't get it — from my perspective you must be very used to people saying nice things about you.'

'Not the predictable 'how have you reached the age of thirty-four without being married' question. Is that the best you can do?'

'Actually, I thought you might want to ask me that boring old question,' he commented.

This was firmer ground. She'd much rather talk about him than herself. 'Oh, I don't have to,' she said, more confident now. 'I know why you're not married. You're as free as a bird.'

He took his eyes away from the road for a moment to glance across at her and she sensed she'd surprised him.

'You're not tied to anything or anybody. Not even an employer. You work where you want and when you want. And until you finish that house, you don't even have to commit yourself to a place to live.'

Now he smiled. 'Have you been talking to my mother?' he asked wryly. 'You're definitely on the same page there. She's convinced I'm never going to finish the house.'

His mother. Catherine fought back a smile of her own at the thought. He'd mentioned his parents and brothers the day they'd met on the beach, but somehow she had never pictured him as part of a family unit. It went against the image of the cosmopolitan and success-ful man of the world.

But then again, he was also a man who would — and could — tackle manual labour, who was happy to spend an evening each week playing chess with an elderly friend and who also volunteered for the lifeboat, putting his own life at risk to save those of strangers.

She suddenly realised how little she knew about him. Really knew about him. He knew everything about her from her school grades to her shoe size, it seemed, yet she didn't even know Sean's birth date.

The internet hadn't been able to tell her anything personal and the little she did know had come from her father. But under the mystery he was somebody's son, somebody's brother.

At one time he'd been a small boy who needed companionship, comfort and caring, and that boy had grown into the most interesting man she'd ever met. One she couldn't ignore — no matter how hard she tried. 'Your mother doesn't want you living in a caravan?'

'Tonight I'm thinking that she's right. Ah, Cathy. I wish my beautiful home was ready.'

Once again she'd meant to correct him — to say she disliked being called 'Cathy', that nobody ever used that name — but somehow the moment had passed.

It was blunt but she wanted to be honest with him and avoid any misunderstanding between them. Their kiss on the beach hadn't been the start of a flirtation that would end in something even more passionate than that encounter had been, tempting as the prospect might be.

'Dinner and the speeches then we can go. Two-and-a-half hours maximum, and I can be back with Dad by ten, as I said I would be.'

That was what she thought.

Sean had no intention of letting her cut the evening short.

Catherine was intriguing and very, very alluring. She was also an intelligent, independent and sophisticated woman and she was as aware of the attraction between them as he was, although she didn't want to acknowledge it.

He wondered what could make her admit it. He had several hours to convince her and the way she'd looked at him in the kitchen was a hint that it might not be too difficult.

'This is kind of a new experience for me,' he commented.

'Oh?' She sounded wary. There was no reason why she should be after stating so boldly her intention of scuttling back home to the safety of her father's cottage.

'Going out with a woman who doesn't want to be with me. And lets me know about it.'

She laughed softly. It was a good sound — she really should laugh more often. It was another challenge he was happy to take up.

'Of course, women usually fall at your feet, don't they? So this is a first.'

It was a first in many ways, he thought as he negotiated a turn in the road. He'd never been so determined to win over a woman as he was with Catherine tonight.

He'd never needed to — if he wanted a brief liaison or a diversion from his business, he'd always seemed to find it. A pleasant experience and absolutely no danger of any emotional entanglement. He could remain — as Catherine had said — entirely uncommitted.

Win over. He smiled to himself. As if it was a one-way street — he the predator, she the prey. Catherine wanted him and all he had to do was get her to admit it to herself — and to him.

'I'm glad you're cheering up, Catherine. You're making me a happy man, do you know that?'

Out of the corner of his eye he saw her fold her arms across her chest. 'OK, tell me. Whatever it is you want to say, go on — say it.' Her voice was sceptical, as if she was waiting for a punchline. If only she knew he was deadly serious.

He waited until he'd pulled into the hotel car park and brought the vehicle to a standstill.

'Four days ago I didn't have a date.

Now I'm not only with a very beautiful woman, even if she doesn't want me to tell her that, but she's also the VIP guest. I've hit the jackpot, which goes to show that good things happen to those who wait.'

Freeing his seatbelt, then hers, he got out and walked around the car to open her door, knowing full well she wouldn't wait for him as a matter of principle.

A woman who didn't like compliments or help. Sure enough, he was only in time to close the door but he carefully placed himself so as to block her way.

'There is just one thing. I've waited and waited and . . . I hate to say this, Catherine but there is one disappointment so far. I've told you how good you look tonight and you've not said one word about me. After I went to so much trouble, getting out all my best gear.'

If he'd hoped to embarrass her, to be rewarded with one of those delicious blushes, he was mistaken. He should have known she wouldn't be so predictable. Instead she tipped back her head and looked into his eyes for a long moment, then she seemed to come to a decision.

'All right. then,' she said before taking a step towards him, then another until they were just inches apart. 'Well, I suppose . . . ' she said eventually, ' . . . as a last-minute replacement, you'll do.'

With one last glance at his face, she tucked her evening bag under her arm, stepped casually around him and walked away towards the hotel entrance. Left alone, Sean let out a low breath, he hadn't even realised he'd forgotten to breathe.

An Evening Ends In Sadness

Catherine felt his presence behind her rather than heard it. Her body was so attuned to his that she could trace every step as his long legs proved more than a match for her high heels.

She hadn't really wanted to get away from him, but the latest move had given her a few precious seconds of breathing space before being once again too close to that overwhelming personality.

The latest move. That made it sound like a game, not so very different from the chess he played with her father once a week. And if that was what it was, where would it end? Where did she want it to end?

Unconsciously she slowed her own pace and within seconds he was beside her, murmuring, 'You don't shake me off that easily, Cathy.'

She glanced at his face, noting the amusement there and a new wave of confusion washed over her. He'd thrown her off-course with his innocent flirting in the car and she hadn't been expecting the fact that they were dressed up and going on what might be perceived to be a date to have such a powerful effect on her ability to think straight.

'I didn't expect to. We had a deal that we would go to the dinner together — so we will.' She liked that. A deal — it put the evening on a business footing once more.

Who are you fooling, Catherine Earnshaw, mocked a voice inside her head. As if you're not thinking almost every moment about that kiss on the beach and the possibility of repeating it.

Except look where that kiss had led — another argument about his cliff-top development and the painful recognition that he wasn't above using his attractiveness to get what he wanted.

'You like a challenge,' he commented.

'It could make for an interesting evening. If you'd let it.'

The next moment she felt his hand on the small of her back, protecting her from the crush of people in the hotel foyer and guiding her slightly in the direction of the uncomfortably named Valentine's Room.

Suddenly she knew how they must look — her height well matched to his, her darkness contrasting with his blond hair, her silver-grey dress complementing his black evening suit. They made an eye-catching couple, she knew, and that was what people would think they were — a couple.

If she had any sense she'd run a mile. Challenge or no challenge, job or no job.

★　★　★

The first person they saw made it impossible to run. Helen Padley was smiling widely, but beneath the welcome Catherine could sense some nervous tension. Helen and her husband, Dave, had taken on the task of organising this year's annual Bridby Lifeboat Dinner, the most important event in the rescue service's year.

'Hi!' Catherine said enthusiastically, kissing her friend. 'Look at everything! You've done a fabulous job, Helen. The room looks amazing.'

'So do you. Both of you.' Helen smiled at Sean, before turning her attention to Catherine. 'The dress was worth it — worth every penny. Honestly, Catherine, you were so right to get it.'

'What? Catherine told me it was just some old thing she threw on.' Sean bent to kiss Helen's cheek and was rewarded with a laugh.

'Are you kidding? Getting the right dress has been the focus of our attention. You don't just 'throw on' something like that.'

'Of course, we never want men to think we've dressed for them, but we always do,' Helen was saying. 'It's true, you know.'

'I hope it is,' he said easily, as if he wanted to forestall the contradiction on Catherine's lips.

'I'm glad you've made it. We've altered the seating arrangements so you're on our table,' Helen said, looking down at the clipboard in her hand. 'Oh — at last. I need this!'

A waitress had appeared at their side with a tray of drinks.

'You deserve it,' Catherine said sympathetically as she watched her friend pick up a glass of champagne before following suit. 'You should have taken yesterday off work — trying to organise this as well as being at the Gazette.'

'I know, I know.'

'And you, sir?' The waitress, a blonde girl, barely old enough to be serving alcohol, was looking up at Sean with bright-eyed appreciation.

Men always looked good in evening suits, Catherine thought, and he looked better than most.

'No alcohol for me, please, I'm

afraid,' he said with the sort of heartbreaking smile that could melt the iciest heart, before taking a glass of water from the back of the tray. The girl returned the smile, then reluctantly moved on to the next group giving him one last lingering glance.

'It's a shame you're on call. But let's hope it's a quiet night and there's nobody who needs rescuing,' Helen said sympathetically.

'I always hope nobody needs rescuing.'

Catherine found her eyes drawn irresistibly to his face at the quietly spoken words. The lifeboat had fascinated her as a child — growing up by the sea she knew its power and her imagination had been fired by the men who risked their lives by leaving the safety of dry land to go to the aid of others in danger. And they were all volunteers.

Knowing that Sean was one of those men puzzled her. He was a newcomer to the town yet he was now part of that tight-knit group who risked life and limb on behalf of strangers.

He'd been brought up by the water, he'd told her of his childhood in Northern Ireland the day they'd met on the beach, but there was something about his involvement with the lifeboat crew that puzzled her.

For all his confident charm, she knew that Sean was a loner — independent and self-contained. In the car she'd accused him of being committed to nothing except himself, and it didn't make sense that he would involve himself in an organisation that demanded not only teamwork but the ultimate commitment from its volunteers.

But these were dangerous thoughts. She didn't want to think too deeply about the person below the surface because she had enough trouble dealing with the glossy surface itself. He was so attractive and if she started to like him, too, she could really be in trouble.

Come on, she chided herself as she listened to him chat casually with Helen. You're not here to moon over a man, especially not this one.

Keep your distance and think about the speech you have to give. You should be worrying about that, not about what Sean Radford-Jones is thinking and feeling.

'Right — I'll leave you two to entertain yourselves,' Helen said suddenly and with one last smile she was gone, consulting her clipboard every few seconds in her eagerness to make her arrangements a success.

So much for keeping her distance.

Left alone with him, Catherine took another sip of champagne to snatch a moment to compose herself. 'There are lots of people Dad knows here. He would have enjoyed this,' she said neutrally, glancing around the room.

'Maybe. Bill looked tired tonight.'

She shot him a quick glance and frowned slightly. 'Yes, I thought that. I hope he's had an early night, though he said he was going to do the 'homework' from his local history class. Not that he ever does it — the homework, I mean.

He seems to love going to the classes, but he's not so keen when it comes to reading or researching things by himself.'

Sean smiled. He at least was perfectly at ease as he reached out to pluck another glass of champagne from a passing waiter's tray, exchanging it for her empty one. 'Twenty years ago I'm thinking he was the one worrying about someone not doing her homework.'

She took the drink but hesitated for a moment before putting the glass to her lips. 'Oh no, I always did my homework. I was a very careful student.'

'Why does that not surprise me? Do you ever behave badly?'

She'd been asking herself that question all evening. And she still didn't have the answer. Fortunately she was saved the trouble of replying.

'Sean! Good to see you. And Catherine.'

'Hey, Neville.'

She shouldn't feel disappointed because Neville Bradshaw, the lifeboat operations manager and host for the evening, had walked up to speak to them. She shouldn't feel disappointed, but she did.

Neville — a pleasant, quiet man in his late 30s — greeted Sean with a handshake and Catherine with a kiss.

'I'm glad you were able to come tonight. Your support means a lot to the lifeboat station. And your generosity.'

'The Gazette's, you mean.'

'Yes, but it never happened with the previous editor. I noticed you've been making some changes to the paper. You're doing a great job from what I can see — and I'm not saying that because you're planning to do a weekly feature on us!'

Watching her, Sean saw that Catherine was pleased by the compliment. She was more comfortable receiving praise for her work than her appearance, he thought, which was all well and good, but she needed to know how desirable she was as well as clever and professional.

'Sean's being very modest,' Neville

was saying. 'He didn't want to be in your newspaper as the first of your profiles on the lifeboat crews. I'm not sure why. We think he's our best advertisement for the service. Don't you agree?'

'Everybody has a story to tell,' she said diplomatically.

Sean thrust his hands into his pockets and allowed himself a small smile. She would do anything rather than admit any personal connection between them, which amused him greatly.

The more distance she tried to place between them, the more sure he was that the attraction was mutual. Otherwise she would be as natural with him as she was with other people.

She wasn't immune to him, whatever she liked to pretend, and that was why he wouldn't let her elude him any longer.

He realised how much he enjoyed watching her as she chatted with Neville, sipping her champagne and talking knowledgeably on a range of subjects.

It was the same when the conversation included other people. Everybody, it seemed wanted to talk to them — about the evening ahead, about the lifeboat, about the development and most of all about the Gazette.

That was the moment when he realised the evening really was a first for him. For the first time in his life he, Sean Radford-Jones, was playing second fiddle to his date. Catherine was more important than he was, as he'd told her in the car, a VIP guest and he was merely her date.

The lucky guy chosen to accompany her and be everything expected of the perfect escort — polite, charming and utterly unthreatening.

He was, he realised with chagrin, just there for show. He'd thought he was doing her such a favour — it had been so amusing to step into Bill's shoes and offer to take her to the dinner.

How gallant, how generous he had been to poor Catherine to take her out when nobody else wanted to — or so he'd thought. But it seemed the joke was on him after all.

Catherine didn't need a date — she would have attended the dinner just as happily with her father by her side, or even alone. She didn't need him, just as she didn't need that tiny evening bag she was clutching in one hand.

Another accessory she could take or leave as the mood demanded. How flattering. How ironic. The miracle was that he didn't care, though he did care when they drifted apart and found themselves in separate conversations. It was what people did at such events, of course — they were sociable, they spoke to other people, they chatted and they smiled.

'I really admire your work.'

The voice brought him back down to earth. He blinked and turned his gaze on the man standing beside him, drink in hand, as they surveyed the crowded room.

He trawled his memory for the man's name — something to do with the abbey . . . yes, the manager at Bridby's historic abbey. He remembered his receptionist, Bernice, telling him something more about the man. Trub . . . yes, Simon Trub.

'I've seen the model of your development,' the man was saying. 'It's what this town has needed for a long time. When will you be starting work?'

'We don't have planning permission yet.'

A memory of Catherine's cool appraisal of his work, the perceptive questions she'd asked and the damning simplicity of her final opinion — progress at all costs. It wasn't true and she knew it — hiding behind her professional persona to mask her real longings . . .

'That's a formality,' Simon Trub said confidently. 'It's the council's project. They're not going to refuse permission, are they?'

'It's a project from the regeneration and development department. But it's the elected members who will make the decision in the end. I'm only the hired hand.'

'I know there are some members

against it — for whatever reason. Don't they see the town has to develop or fade away?'

'There's nothing wrong with healthy debate,' Sean said easily, thinking where he'd heard those words before.

Then wanting to move the conversation on, he searched for something to say when he really wasn't interested at all. 'So, you'll be preparing for the busiest time of the year, I guess.'

'Hmm, yes. This summer will be busier than ever. We're having a Shakespeare festival in August, with performances every night in the abbey grounds. It's the first time we'll have opened in the evenings.'

'Sounds interesting,' he said, when he meant the exact opposite.

'It's a great idea. Catherine suggested it.'

Now that was interesting. Suddenly all his senses were on alert. 'Catherine?'

'Catherine Earnshaw. The editor of the Gazette . . . ' the man began, glancing around the room, but Sean cut him off mid-sentence.

Suddenly he found he didn't like the implication that another man could introduce him to Catherine. That this man had a prior claim on her attention — or even her acquaintance.

'I didn't know you knew Catherine,' he said casually, reclaiming his position as the man closest to her.

'We both serve on the summer festival committee. She's a real asset to the Gazette — to the whole town.'

'I'll tell her you said so,' Sean said smoothly. 'We're here together tonight, and I know she'll be interested in what you say. In fact . . . if you'll excuse me, I think I need to go back to my date.'

★ ★ ★

OK, what was behind that show of macho posturing, he asked himself as he walked away. There was something about the man's manner that had irritated him.

So they were on the same committee,

were they? Well, so what. First name terms already . . . But was that any business of his? Simon Trub was a soon-to-be-divorced father-of-three and if he liked Catherine and she liked him what did it have to do with him, Sean, anyway?

The thought shocked him with its ferocity. If anyone were going to kiss Catherine tonight it would be him, he thought darkly. Maybe — if he was lucky or he provoked her into it — she would initiate the kiss.

He knew she could be reckless and that she wasn't immune to him — however much she tried to pretend otherwise — and there was something about her that meant he would go to any lengths to ensure he was the one she was reckless with.

He wanted everyone to know she was with him. There was no way Simon Trub or any other of the 100 or so men present would think they stood a chance of getting close to Catherine while he was around.

For one thing, he told himself, her father had entrusted her into his care. OK, she was a highly intelligent career woman who took great pains to show everyone that she didn't need to be in anyone's care but the principle was there. He wasn't just her date, he was . . . almost part of the family.

He headed across the room in her direction. She was talking with several people he vaguely recognised but that didn't bother him. It was Catherine who was the focus of his attention tonight.

When a familiar and rather shapely blonde stepped in his way, it was an irritation he could have done without.

'Hi, Sean. It's good to see you.'

'Hey there.'

He couldn't ignore her but his smile didn't quite reach his eyes. Diane Minton was a solicitor who worked for the council and their paths had crossed professionally as part of his work on the development.

He knew she was divorced and he also knew that she liked him. She was attractive, intelligent and fun — and the last person he wanted to speak to because she was standing between Catherine and himself.

There was only one woman he was interested in and it wasn't this one.

'You'll have to excuse me, Diane,' he said with what he hoped was his most winning smile. 'There's somebody I need to speak to. I'll catch you later.'

He wouldn't, but she wasn't to know that. Instead he grabbed a glass of champagne from a passing waitress and walked straight up to Catherine, giving just a cursory nod to the two people she had been in conversation with before turning her gaze on the room around her.

Without a word he repeated his action of earlier — taking the empty glass from her hand before replacing it with a full one.

He saw her take a deep breath. 'Where did you appear from?' she said after a moment's hesitation.

'I noticed your glass was empty, and I

couldn't leave you without a drink,' he said with a smile, and this time it was genuine.

'That's very kind of you. Very . . . gallant.'

That was the word he'd used in his own mind. 'I thought you might need it.'

'Ahead of my speech, you mean?'

'Do you? Do you need it?'

The people she had been speaking to had drifted away and there could have been just the two of them in the room as she looked at him, eyes bright. How had he never really noticed those beautiful grey eyes?

He remembered saying she was beautiful to tease her the first time they'd met at her dad's house, but she was. In every way.

Especially when she was self-conscious. He watched the colour wash over her face and she ignored his question.

'You're not trying to get me drunk, are you?' she asked with a slight smile.

'Would it work if I was?'

She held his gaze for several seconds then shrugged her shoulders.

OK, now that wasn't what he was expecting. From previous experience he knew Catherine had no reservations about speaking her mind. Which meant . . .

'On what?'

'On whether I decide to keep to my ten o'clock curfew.'

He was saved from having to think up a reply to that by the awareness that people were taking their seats for dinner and the chance for a private conversation had disappeared.

But he was making progress, so he didn't mind them sitting down with three other couples for the meal and easily joined in the general conversation, all the time aware that eventually they would be alone again and she would have to make that choice.

*   *   *

If the subject was troubling her, she gave no sign of it during the meal. She

148

ate with good appetite and chatted to their fellow guests as if she didn't have a care in the world.

She seemed quite at home with him by her side, which was a minor triumph after her efforts to keep him at arm's length. Of course she was with her friends and he remembered Helen Padley's words at the garage.

It was something to think about — how different the professional and inspiring editor Helen had described was from the Catherine of Bill Earnshaw's memories . . . the tomboy with the scrapes on her knees, the little girl forever with her nose in a book, the teenager who dreamed of travelling to far-off places . . .

After the meal, it was time for the formalities of the evening — and Catherine's big moment. When Neville Bradshaw stepped on the small stage set up at one end of the room, she got up without a word and moved to stand behind him.

Sean settled back in his seat and

waited. This would be interesting. He knew about the Gazette sponsorship of the lifeboat and the plan for the fundraising campaign, of course, but he was intrigued to hear what else she had to say. And how she said it.

She was good. Very good. She said all the right things — thanked all the right people, spoke eloquently about the role of the lifeboat service and its importance, and finally announced the sponsorship deal — and all without notes or a prompt.

If she hadn't pushed several strands of hair behind her ear he would never have known she was nervous. And that made it all the more impressive.

He got to his feet when she returned to the table, holding out her chair without a word. She flashed him a slight smile, but someone across the table was already asking her a question, claiming her attention

Out of the corner of his eye, he saw a small scrap of paper flutter down to the floor and he stooped to pick it up.

He glanced down at the words — *thanks, history, volunteers, bravery, sponsorship, good wishes* — and he realised that her speech hadn't been quite so off the cuff after all. Not that there was anything wrong with that.

He slipped the paper into his pocket before retaking his seat and leaning back to listen to the conversation across the table. Beside him, Catherine also seemed to be happy to merely listen, but when a few minutes later he saw her turn her head and surreptitiously look about her he knew exactly what she was seeking.

Resting one hand on the back of her chair, he leant forward with deceptive casualness and whispered in her ear, 'It's all right — it's in my pocket.'

When her eyes met his, there was surprise there and something else. Somehow it amused and touched him that she would write keyword reminders on a scrap of paper so small nobody else would even imagine she was holding it in her hand.

And he felt something he had never expected to feel for any woman, let alone a woman like Catherine Earnshaw. For some reason he felt protective towards her.

She was a woman of many shades and the ones he liked best were the ones few people saw. He liked her when she blushed and fiddled nervously with her hair, or said things she didn't mean.

He also liked it when she laughed, spoke of her childhood or joked with her dad, revealing that there was so much more to her than the composed and confident journalist.

Across the table, Helen Padley watched them with amusement and blatant interest. Catherine, turning away from Sean's penetrating gaze, found her attention caught by her friend's open scrutiny.

In its own way it was just as uncomfortable because there was a definite smugness in Helen's expression. But she didn't care. For the first time in a long time she really did not care what anybody else thought. She was having too good a time to worry about that.

* * *

Catherine didn't know at what point she'd realised she was enjoying herself. It could have been during the conversation in the car park, or maybe it was when she and Sean walked into the hotel and she realised she was glad she was with him.

As dates went, she had to admit that he would more than 'do'. In fact, she was the one who'd hit the jackpot, as he'd called it.

He was the perfect companion — gorgeous, intelligent and interesting, charming but not a charmer — and she wondered again why he hadn't had a date for this evening before she'd been handed to him on a platter. Did he expect whichever lucky woman he chose to be waiting for him right up until the last minute? Or to drop any other plans she may have made?

He was so confident, so sure of himself, and there was something exciting about her welfare being in his hands.

She'd watched those hands as they poured glasses of wine for her and water for himself, and the way his tanned skin had contrasted with the pure white of the cloth as he rested one palm on the table.

He was making her feel special — and she hadn't felt special in a long time. She liked the way he was attentive without being overpowering, and the way he'd got to his feet when she rose to leave the table ahead of her speech. He had beautiful manners and she liked that. She liked him.

She'd felt rather than seen him watching her from across the room while he was talking to the man from the abbey and had felt a shiver down her spine — even 20 yards across a crowded room. It was a cliché but their whole relationship had been a series of clichés. Everything she'd ever dreamed of was embodied in this man and she didn't know whether to be elated or scared.

He was so . . . so . . . special.

Excusing herself for a moment, she found the Gazette photographer finishing his coffee on another table and organised pictures for both the newspaper and the lifeboat organisation to keep.

She smiled widely the one time she agreed to be in front of the camera, then left young Neil to his job and returned to her own table. Most people had moved away but Sean was waiting there, standing with hands in pockets as he leant back against the table and surveyed the room.

'Only one photograph?' he asked with a smile, watching as she picked up her evening bag.

'I think one picture of the editor is enough.'

'I thought you would want to be the star of the show. Otherwise I'll think you really did wear that dress just for me, Cathy.'

Whether he remembered the kiss or not, he was certainly flirting with her again. There was the lazy smile, the warm and slightly challenging note in his voice as he said the nickname he only ever used when they were alone — not to mention the look in his eyes. But this time she didn't mind at all. In fact . . .

'Of course I did,' she said with a smile. The relief of having finished her speech relaxed her. Maybe that was why she could say what wanted to. 'Everything I do is aimed at impressing you, Sean, and it seems to be working.'

The gleam in his eyes became brighter. 'It is tonight.'

She'd known what he'd thought, she'd felt it, the moment they'd first laid eyes on each other that evening. She'd known that they had become attracted to each other.

She swallowed and every word in the English language went out of her head.

She might have been struck dumb because she honestly could not think of a single thing to say. Except 'yes', whispered a voice somewhere inside her.

She was so attracted to him it almost hurt and though she knew there could never be a future for her with him, she couldn't help but imagine what it would be like to give in to that attraction.

It would be the most reckless thing she'd done. She'd never been crazy like other women. She'd always played safe. Even as a teenager she'd been too focussed on becoming a journalist, too wrapped up in her fantasies of a literary hero, to be like other girls.

She hadn't backpacked around Europe that summer before university, or partied all night instead of studying when she did make it to college. She was too serious, too ambitious and under it all, too romantic to act first and think about the consequences later.

And where had it got her? A great job that meant spending 10 hours a day at the office — and when she did leave, she'd go home to an empty flat. Not even a cat to keep her company, certainly no-one to spend lazy Sundays with or to curl up against on cold winter evenings.

She'd been waiting so long for that romantic hero to sweep her off her feet that she'd forgotten how to live in the meantime.

He was watching her with a trace of a smile on his face as if he could read her every thought. He'd always been one step ahead but she didn't care about that anymore. All she cared about was . . .

A faint sound coming from her evening bag broke into her reverie and she reached inside for her phone. She had meant to call her father but she'd forgotten about that because — well, the only thing she had been thinking of was listening to her body not her mind for once. But she'd phone him now — after this call, whatever it was.

Sean knew immediately that something was wrong. He knew it from the way her whole body stilled and her face drained of its colour before his eyes. He'd been enjoying the flush on her cheeks and the glint in her eyes.

But not anymore. Like the coldest of cold showers, something had put out the fire. In an instant Catherine could have been turned to stone as she listened then spoke a few brief words into the handset before ending the call. He stepped forward so they were so close they were almost touching. 'What is it? What's happened?' he asked urgently.

She looked at him with more pain in her eyes than he'd ever seen before. 'It's Dad. He's had a heart attack.'

'He Shouldn't Have Been Alone'

The world swung on its axis and for a moment even he — cool, level-headed, always-in-control Sean Radford-Jones — forgot where he was. Then everything came back into focus including Catherine, who was standing there as if turned to stone.

'Come on.' He grabbed her hand and headed for the door without even a sideways glance at the rest of the room. He barely even noticed that Catherine's fingers had curled around his own, except that he tightened his grip in a vague effort to offer comfort.

'Ah, Bill. I don't believe it,' he said almost to himself as they crossed the car park. Thank God he had the car and that he had drunk only mineral water all evening. Though this news would have sobered him up anyway.

He held the door as she got in, in a repeat gesture of just a few hours earlier. But this time, when he took his own seat and put the engine into gear, his words to her were very different.

'He's at the hospital? Bridby General?'

'Yes. They've taken him to Accident and Emergency.' Catherine's voice was quiet, subdued.

'Who was it on the phone?' he asked, glancing at her profile in the half-light of the car. Any softness was gone now — her features were drawn in harsh, rigid lines. The golden glow of the evening had faded to nothing, the dream date had become a nightmare.

'It was the paramedic,' she said in something like despair. 'Dad called the ambulance himself. Because he was alone, he called the ambulance himself . . .'

Sean bit down on his lip, but he said nothing. Instead he concentrated on the road ahead of him. The country road was dark and quiet, twisting its way to the lights of the town in the distance.

'I shouldn't have come tonight.'

'Don't say that . . . '

'You said it yourself — he looked tired. He looked . . . ill and I didn't notice and instead came out to talk to a roomful of people I don't know.'

'Catherine.'

She turned to face him, eyes full of unshed tears, which was so unlike her that it shook him even more than her words had.

He reached out to touch her hand briefly as it rested on the evening bag in her lap, but he had to release his hold to steer the car into the hospital car park. He didn't know what to say, anyway.

They left the car in silence, but without thinking he took her hand once more and led the way into the Accident and Emergency department. Not the best place to be on a Saturday night. Not the best place to be anytime.

'Can I help?' The woman at the

reception desk looked up as they approached and Catherine forced herself to speak.

She had to pull herself together when all she wanted to do was bury herself in Sean Radford-Jones's arms and cry like she hadn't cried for years. Not since her mother had died, and she didn't want to think about that tonight. Not while her dad was ill. Oh Dad . . .

'My father was brought in by ambulance,' she said quietly. 'He's had a heart attack. Bill Earnshaw — William Earnshaw.'

'Oh yes. The doctors are looking at him now.'

Just a normal evening at work for the hospital staff. It was so easy for them to be businesslike and professional whereas she was falling apart . . . The receptionist looked up from the computer screen and handed her a sheet of paper. 'Can you fill this in, with your father's details?'

Catherine looked around for a pen, the empty holder on the reception desk telling its own story.

Normally she never went anywhere without a pen — her very first editor had said no proper journalist ever did — but that wretched evening bag was just too small. She heard a click and Sean handed her a pen, primed ready to use.

He'd taken it from an inside pocket of his jacket and somehow the slight warmth from the intimate contact with his body reassured her.

He waited while she filled in the form, a silent but comforting presence beside her.

'I'm not sure of his doctor's phone number,' she said to the receptionist as she handed back the form.

'Who is it? Oh, Dr Linden. We'll fill that part in. If you want to take a seat, someone will let you know when there's some news.'

'Take a seat,' she murmured, clutching her bag as they walked over to a row of plain plastic chairs. 'Why can't people say what they mean? Why can't they say 'sit down'? That's what they mean so just say it.'

She felt his eyes on her as they sat down side by side. 'Yeah. Wouldn't life be simpler?'

Catherine didn't think life would ever be simple again. 'I wonder how long it will be,' she said slowly, gazing at the unfamiliar scene around her.

* * *

The Accident and Emergency department was quiet for a Saturday night. There were three dishevelled men congregating around a television showing highlights of a football match, one of them bearing a head wound that probably looked worse than it was. There was a scattering of other people without any visible sign of injury: maybe they, too, were waiting for someone. Or for some news . . . any news . . .

Sean shrugged slightly and thrust his hands into his pockets as he stretched his legs out in front of him. 'Who knows? I guess there's no set time. Depends on so many things.'

'I'm not used to this.'

'Why should you be? It's not something you plan for.' He paused for a moment and she felt his eyes on her. 'You OK?'

She nodded then shook her head. 'Mum was diagnosed at this hospital,' she said quietly and she felt Sean go still beside her.

'Your mother?'

She felt his arm around her shoulders and something warm brushed her forehead that could have been a whisper of a kiss.

Whatever it was, it comforted her, telling her she was not alone. 'She responded well to treatment at first. Then it came back and . . . it was very quick.'

'Bill must miss her. And you do, too.'

'Every day.' She thought about it for a moment. 'Mum was always busy. She had the most energy of anyone I've ever known.'

They lapsed into silence and the past and present seemed to collide in her mind. Now it was her dad that was ill and she had to do something practical ... 'I have to phone Lewis,' she said suddenly, turning to look at Sean as if she'd just remembered her brother's very existence.

'It must be ... ' he frowned and glanced down at his watch, 'the middle of night in Dubai.'

'I know, but I need to tell him.'

She fished into her bag and took out the phone then got to her feet. 'I'll have to go outside — they won't let me use it in here. Will you wait?'

Sean had stood up, too, and for a moment she thought he would try to stop her. There was a burst of raucous laughter from the dishevelled men they'd noticed earlier — now just two of them waiting while the third's injuries were attended to — and Sean hesitated as he glanced in their direction.

'Of course I'll wait,' he said eventually. 'Here.' Slipping off his jacket he draped it around her shoulders.

She'd forgotten that she was wearing an evening dress — a short, brief evening dress which was fine for a glitzy dinner but not quite so practical for a hospital casualty department.

'I left my wrap at the hotel.'

'I'll call them tomorrow. Somebody may hand it in.'

'That's all right. I don't care about the wrap.'

She'd much rather wear his jacket anyway. If the pen had felt comforting, then this was better. It was warm and far too big, but the heat of his body seemed to transfer itself to her, seeping through to her chilled bones.

'Be careful out there and come right back. OK?'

She nodded.

'I'll come get you if there's any news.'

She didn't think there would be but it was reassuring to hear him say that. Sean was the rock she was clinging to right now. She was glad of his jacket, too, when she stepped out into the open air to make her call.

She heard the ringing tone across all the miles, its insistent call failing to rouse any response in that desert city except an electronic voice advising her to leave a message.

Although like most expatriates, Lewis Earnshaw had domestic staff, they would have gone for the night. And so, it seemed, had Lewis. He'd never given her a mobile phone number, she thought.

She shivered and slipped her arms into the warmth of Sean's jacket before trying the number again, just in case.

Finally she decided to leave a message, a few brief words and both her mobile number and that at the cottage. Just in case he'd lost it, she thought with a flash of resentment as she wrapped the jacket closer around her. It would be one reason for his lack of communication.

★ ★ ★

When she returned to the Accident and Emergency, Sean was taking a plastic cup from a nearby vending machine. He indicated for her to sit down again while he selected a second drink.

She made no effort to give him back his jacket, instead watching him in his white dress shirt. He'd opened the collar and loosened his bow-tie, which hung in black strands either side of the open neck.

Neither of them had expected this when they'd dressed for the evening, she thought as her eyes rested on the tanned column of his throat. He looked so good, yet she hadn't told him so, which seemed crazy now that real life had intruded on the fantasy. She really wished she'd told him . . .

She forced her attention to his face as he handed her one of the plastic cups.

'Black coffee, right?' He grinned slightly at her surprise. 'It's what you had earlier.'

At the dinner table, when she'd

actually felt happy. 'You're very observant.'

'Artist's eye.'

'I thought you were an architect.'

'I consider what I do to be an art.'

He took his seat beside her but he didn't attempt to touch her again. She wished he would but then again she liked the way they could talk so easily to each another. It was making everything easier.

'What did he say?'

'Lewis? He wasn't there. I left a message, but I don't know when he'll get it.'

'You've done what you can.' He sipped his own coffee, the sighed as he ran a hand through his short blond hair. 'Bill has high blood pressure, right?'

She nodded.

'I knew he took some kind of medication.'

'Each night before he goes to bed. I have to remind him most of the time. He gets very tired — like he was

171

tonight . . . ' Her voice trailed away at the memory and the thought of what was happening somewhere else in the hospital.

'It'll be OK,' he said quietly. 'I don't know about medical things but it seems to me your dad has a lot to live for.'

That clear blue gaze seemed to see right through her. It held sympathy and understanding, and there was no-one else in the world she would rather have with her at that moment, while everything was in such turmoil.

Earlier in the evening that thought would have scared her — now she didn't think she could get through the next few hours without him.

'I should have come home before,' she said into the silence, the thought that had been eating away at her no longer able to be kept inside. 'After Mum died. He shouldn't have been alone.'

'Why are you blaming yourself? Cathy . . . Catherine, this is not your fault.' He reached out to brush a strand of hair away from her face, before pushing it behind her ear. 'No way is this your fault.'

'I barely see him, Sean. You've spent more time with him than I have.'

'Don't beat yourself up over this. I know how close you are to your dad. He thinks the world of you. It's 'Katie this' and 'Katie that'. I was sick of hearing about you long before I ever met you.'

She smiled at that, as he'd meant her to, but the smile didn't reach her eyes or her heart.

Sean took her hand in his own and decided he hated himself. This evening was not tuning out like he'd expected — which was probably just as well.

He'd done nothing but flirt with her, he'd tried to provoke her into admitting she wanted him — and he'd been so sure of his success . . . Now here they were, sitting in an Accident and Emergency department while her father — his friend — was fighting for his life and it was a miracle she could even bear to look at him.

But amazingly she could and her hand held his in so tight a grip that he could not have let go, even if he'd wanted to.

Catherine, who was so confident and sure of herself in her work, so sure of herself and her place in the world, was so vulnerable underneath that icy self-control.

'He's very proud of you, you know that?'

'I don't know why.'

'Because of this,' he said, picking up a rather battered copy of *Elan* magazine from the table beside him with his free hand. She may not have noticed it there among the gardening journals and children's comics, but he had.

He'd seen enough copies of the magazine at Bill's cottage to recognise the cover immediately, and one glance at the date — from the previous summer — told him that it was one of the issues Catherine had edited.

'It's just a magazine. Nothing important. Meant to be thrown away almost as soon as it's printed. It's the same with a newspaper — wrapped around someone's chips almost as soon as the ink is dry.'

'They don't do that anymore. And in any case, this one hasn't been thrown away — it's more than a year old.'

'A year!' She shook her head in self-deprecation. 'It's hardly a good reason not to be here when my dad needed me.'

The sound of three rough male voices disturbed them and they lapsed into silence as the three men — one now with a bandage wrapped around the crown of his head — stumbled their way out of the Accident and Emergency.

He saw her shiver and felt another pang of concern. 'Are you warm enough?'

She nodded but wrapped his jacket closer around her. 'Dad's right. This dress is ridiculous.'

Oh Catherine . . . 'You know what I think of your dress.' He regretted being so calculating but he couldn't deny that his attraction to her was genuine.

'You're not the one wearing it.'

That was more like the Catherine Earnshaw he knew.

'It looks better on you — you know it does. Just as you know that you're not to blame for any of this. Come on — I've seen you when you're at work, like tonight. You're confident in what you do, Catherine.'

'It's all a façade,' she said with brutal honesty. 'I'm just a very average person hiding behind the image, waiting to be found out.'

He made a small sound in denial of that statement. 'Even when you were Editor of the Year?'

'At the second time of asking.'

'Yeah, and after being voted Feature Writer of the Year three years running . . .'

She stared at him in something like surprise.

'Your dad,' he explained. 'But I looked you up on the internet, too. I don't think there's anything average about you — and that's the final compliment you're getting until you pay me one back.'

She smiled slightly at the ironic reference to their earlier conversation and looked down at their linked hands.

'There's so much I wanted to do. The house — you've seen it. It's falling apart. And the garden. It was never like that when Mum was alive.'

'Your mum was the gardener, right?'

'Mmm.'

'I didn't think it was Bill. He likes to sit out there and do his crosswords. And fall asleep, I think.'

Her whole face softened. A pleasant memory at last. 'Yes, he does . . . '

'I remember last autumn, finding him asleep in that chair . . . So you're a gardener, too, huh?'

She shook her head. 'In a first-floor flat in north London? But it's something I want to do more of. I'm sorry.'

He frowned at that. 'For what? Not being an expert gardener?'

'For feeling so sorry for myself and being so needy.'

'There's nothing wrong with being upset about your dad. I like Bill. He's a good man.'

She might have known he would still reassure her. That was why she was desperately glad he was with her. That and the fact he was holding her hand so tightly, rubbing his thumb the length of hers whenever he spoke.

He had nice hands — an artist's hands. She remembered the sketch he'd shown her on the beach. With just a few strokes of a pencil he'd created a startling and compelling image of the abbey, and she wondered if he drew people as well as buildings.

Was that too personal? Was he really so uncommitted, as she'd accused him earlier, that he didn't even get close to people through his art?

'He said that about you, too,' she said slowly. 'I'm so pleased he met you. You've no idea . . . '

She sensed he was about to say

something — maybe something profound, but once more a noise disturbed their private conversation. It was the sound of footsteps as someone walked down the corridor towards them and they both turned to watch the person — a man in a white coat, presumably a doctor.

His steps echoed in the near-empty department and Catherine held her breath as he approached. But the footsteps didn't slow and the man walked past them without a word.

'False alarm,' she whispered, as she watched him disappear into the distance.

'It could be hours yet.'

'I know.'

'Do you want another coffee?' He waved away her attempt to pick up her bag. 'I'll get it. You're my date tonight so it's my job, right?'

His date. How long ago did that seem? An eternity . . . She watched him at the machine again and accepted her coffee with thanks this time. 'How often do you go home?' she asked when he was seated back beside her.

'To Belfast?'

She nodded.

'Two, three times a year. Always at Christmas and I stop off there sometimes if I'm travelling with the job. Like when I was in San Diego last month.'

She gazed at him, admiring his profile and the way the corners of his mouth curled up ever so slightly when he was thinking of something pleasant.

'Belfast isn't on the way back to Bridby from anywhere, let alone California,' she pointed out.

He shrugged. 'There's always connecting flights through London. I like to go back to Belfast Lough, to visit.'

To visit. But he lived in Bridby — for now.

'And your mother wants you to finish the house.'

That brought a wry smile to his face.

'Yeah. She wants me to put down roots someplace and she doesn't think I should be living in a caravan. You have a lot in common.'

Catherine wasn't so sure, but she liked the softness in his voice when he spoke of his mother. It was hard to imagine him as part of a loving family — he was so independent, so in control of everything he did. But then again, she hadn't understood his involvement with the sea rescue service either.

'What does she think about you volunteering for the lifeboat?' she asked curiously. 'She must worry about you.'

'She would — if she knew.'

'You haven't told her?'

'You said yourself, she'd worry. What she doesn't know can't hurt her.'

'Well, yes. Except . . . ' Her voice trailed away as she thought about what he'd said. 'What if something happened — if you were hurt?'

'She couldn't change that, even if she knew about the lifeboat.'

'No, but . . . She'd find out about it from strangers, Sean.'

From strangers. For some reason he felt he'd been hit somewhere in the solar plexus.

Most people were strangers to him, he thought. He had friends — people he was friendly with, he supposed — but mostly he was surrounded by strangers. And that was fine for everyday life: no responsibilities, no ties, nothing between him and the ends of the earth if that was where he wanted to go.

Yes, fine for everyday life, but maybe not so great when times weren't so good and you needed someone to give you reassurance and comfort.

Like he was somehow giving Catherine comfort right now.

He suddenly realised he shouldn't be holding her hand. Not when his desire for her was so strong it could make him lose all reason. It wasn't fair — like it hadn't been fair to tease and provoke her, to spend all evening trying to lure her into doing something she blatantly didn't want to.

★ ★ ★

The sound of someone walking towards them once more disturbed his thoughts and this time the middle-aged man in the white slowed his pace until he was standing directly in front of them.

'You're here for William Earnshaw?' he asked abruptly.

Catherine nodded and her grip on his hand tightened.

'I can tell you he's doing very well. He's conscious and his breathing's getting back to normal. We're very pleased with his progress.'

'He's all right?' she breathed.

The medical staff's pleasure was nothing to Catherine's, Sean thought, watching the way her face lit up and her eyes softened at the news.

'Yes. He's very tired. We'll let him rest tonight and transfer him to the cardiac care unit in the morning. Well . . . ' The doctor glanced down at the watch on his wrist. 'Later this morning, I suppose.'

'But he's going to be all right?'

'Yes. They'll tell you more tomorrow

— he'll need an electrocardiogram of course, but they'll be able to tell you more.'

'Can we go and see him?'

'Of course. Straight through the double doors, then left.'

'Thank you. Thank you so much, doctor.'

Left alone with her, Sean took both Catherine's hands in his and looked down into her pale face, now infused with happiness and relief.

'So, what do you think of that?' he asked with a grin.

He really wanted to laugh at the new brightness in her eyes, the animation in her face now the fear was gone.

'I can't believe he's going to be all right!' she exclaimed. 'I was so worried about him, I can't tell you.'

'I know.'

'He was unconscious when they found him and I know that's bad. Oh, I'm so relieved!'

'Come on.' The words were the ones he'd used when he'd practically dragged her out of the function room at the hotel.

They hadn't even told anyone where they were going, he realised now, in their haste to get to the hospital. But Bill was going to be OK and Catherine was happy again, so nothing else mattered and this time they walked side by side, though still hand in hand.

* * *

Bill Earnshaw was in a bed, an oxygen mask on his ashen face, with a young male nurse hovering nearby. Catherine gave a slight gasp at the sight of him then rushed over to his bedside.

'Oh Dad,' she said. Just two words that spoke of her shock at the sight of him so weak, so vulnerable, but also of her relief after the tension of the long, long evening.

Behind the mask, the elderly man's lips moved in what could have been an attempt at a smile or to form a few words, but Catherine reached over to touch his hair as she sank into a chair beside the bed and gathered one hand between both her own.

The old man's weak gaze — he was without his glasses — focussed on his Catherine and his pleasure was obvious. Sean stepped back slightly with the male nurse to give father and daughter some time alone.

'His daughter? He's been asking for her,' the nurse said quietly.

'They're very close.' Sean thrust his hands into his pockets and watched them, pooled in the light from a bedside lamp. 'Is this a warning — or something more serious?'

The nurse hesitated for a moment, then shrugged his shoulders. 'He was fortunate the paramedics were there quickly, but Dr Williamson says the prognosis is good,' he said eventually.

'Bill's a lucky man.' He'd said those words once before but he couldn't remember when. Oh yeah — the first night he'd seen Catherine at their home and watched her as she read . . .

He watched her now for a few minutes, not wanting to disturb her but knowing they had to go, and eventually he murmured a word of thanks to the nurse as he stepped forward to the bed.

Catherine glanced around at his approach and spoke softly once more. 'It's all right, Dad. You need to sleep. We'll see you tomorrow. I'll bring you what you need. It's all right.'

Bill's gaze slipped past his daughter and his lips moved again.

'I'll take her home, Bill,' Sean said, moving forward to touch her shoulder through the oversized jacket. 'You just get yourself better.'

Catherine leant over to brush her lips against her father's forehead. 'Sleep well, Dad,' she murmured. 'Sleep well.'

Bill Earnshaw's eyelids were already beginning to close so there was nothing left to do but leave him, with another brief word of thanks to the nurse.

Catherine walked slowly this time, pulling the lapels of the jacket together to wrap it closer around her, which meant Sean could avoid taking her hand once more. It wasn't that he didn't want to — he did — but it wouldn't be fair to her. It was time he showed her a little respect.

'I left your pen on the desk,' she said into the quiet as the crossed the moonlit car park.

He shrugged. A pen. As if a pen was worth worrying about.

'And I've worn your jacket longer than you have . . . '

'That's all right. Your need is greater than mine, since you insisted on wearing that ridiculous dress.'

That long-overdue respect didn't mean he couldn't tease her slightly and in return he got the first genuine smile she'd ever given him. It was a beautiful smile made even more beautiful because it was for him and him alone.

'You said you liked it,' she pointed out as he activated the door remote.

'I do. But I don't recommend it as hospital-visiting-wear.'

'I don't suppose you expected to be

driving all over the countryside tonight,' she commented as he climbed into the driver's seat beside her and took a deep breath. 'Now you have to drive past your place to get to the cottage.'

'I know but remember, I promised your dad I'd get you home safely. I'm a man of my word, so let's go.'

★ ★ ★

Catherine watched the shadows passing the windows as they drove through the sleeping town. She felt as if she'd lived a lifetime in one evening — highs and lows and all the other bits in between.

Catherine Earnshaw — Editor of the Year, as Sean had called her — had learnt something about herself tonight. All that success, that control, meant nothing when it came to matters of life and death. Or the heart. And she couldn't pretend to be an expert in those.

She certainly couldn't pretend that to Sean Radford-Jones, but she didn't care. She didn't even mind that she'd lost control of her emotions in front of him. He cared about her dad too and he'd been so kind . . . so . . .

'Here we are.'

She started. She'd been gazing sightlessly at the streets and houses and she hadn't realised that they were home. That the evening was finally at an end.

A Shoulder To Cry On

Suddenly she couldn't bear the thought that Sean might go. Too much had happened — they needed to talk about, to relieve the tension now the emergency was over. She didn't want him to say goodnight and drive away. She wanted to tell him how she felt and how she couldn't have coped without him tonight.

'Please come in for a minute,' she asked. Clumsy but what else she could say?

'Do you need more coffee?' he sounded careful.

'I think I need something. You can't leave without coffee — or tea if you like. I suppose you're still on duty . . . '

He blinked as if he'd forgotten about that. That wasn't like him — Sean Radford-Jones was a man who covered all the bases. Surely nothing would shake him enough to loosen his grip on everything around him?

'Sure,' he said and cut the engine, making sure this time that he was there to open the door for her as she got out of the car. It was the least he could do, though he wasn't sure he was doing the right thing in seeing her right into her home. Things had seemed very simple a few hours ago but they weren't simple any longer.

'I'm so tired,' she commented as she set down her evening bag on the countertop in the kitchen.

But Catherine seemed unperturbed as she filled the automatic kettle and found two mugs from an eye-level cupboard. Setting them down for a moment, she sniffed then moved towards the door. 'I won't be a minute,' she said.

With that she was gone and he heard the bathroom door close softly. If it had been earlier he might have thought she was retouching her make-up but the evening had definitely gone in another direction. Which was no bad thing, he thought.

After several minutes, watching the kettle emit enough steam to fill a small sauna before finally switching itself off, he began to worry where she was. He went up the stairs as quietly as he could and stood outside the closed door to the bathroom.

'Catherine?' he asked. No sound.

He knocked then and after several long moments the door opened. Catherine stood there — still wearing his jacket over her dress, but barefoot now. But it wasn't just the loss of a few inches in height that was making her look smaller and more vulnerable than ever before.

He was appalled to see tears in her eyes — and even more appalled when one trickled down her cheek, closely followed by another.

'Hey . . . ' he said softly.

'I'm sorry.' She tried to smile but it turned into a grimace. 'I didn't want you to see . . . '

Did she think he was that callous, that uncaring, that she didn't want to cry for her dad in front of him? 'Cathy,' he began but as she wiped the tears off her face she interrupted him.

'I don't cry nicely. Some people look fine — or even look great — when they're crying but I don't. I look . . . crumpled and awful.'

It was true. It wasn't the best look on her. Not that she could ever look 'awful' to him and he reached out to brush away another stray tear.

'Like I care about that,' he said gently, trying to coax a smile out of her because it really tore at him to see her in such distress.

She pulled away. 'I'm sorry,' she said again, standing up straight. She slipped the jacket off her shoulders and held it out to him, chin tilted defiantly against whatever she was fighting right now.

After a moment he took it. 'You didn't even want to come in to the house. I'm sorry I forced the issue but I'll be fine now. Thanks for everything.

I'll call you tomorrow and let you know how Dad is. But I think I need to get some rest too. Goodnight.'

With that, she walked past him and headed for what he assumed was her bedroom. He hesitated for a moment. He'd had quite a night and this outpouring of emotion wasn't something he was used to.

He could walk away right now — he knew the way out — and return to the solitude of his caravan. He'd done all he could. She didn't want him to do anything more.

Tossing his jacket over the banister rail, he knocked on the door beyond which he could see a silvery figure outlined against the shadows.

'Catherine,' he said softly, and the moonlight illuminated her tear-streaked face as she turned to him.

'I thought . . . I thought you'd gone.'

'Come back down to the kitchen.' Taking her hand he led her back downstairs.

At that moment real life intervened

in the shape — or sound — of a ringing phone. Keeping hold of Catherine, Sean reached out to grab her bag, flipped it open and handed her the mobile. He listened with unashamed interest as she answered the call.

'No, you didn't wake me,' she said without emotion. 'Where were you, Lewis? No, it doesn't matter. I need to tell you about Dad.'

The absent brother. Better late than never, Sean thought darkly, as Catherine continued to speak into the phone. He could sense the tension in her body, despite the calmness of her voice.

'I don't know. I can't say when Dad can call you,' she was saying. 'The doctors will be there, they said he needs tests. I can't say he has to call you at a certain time because I don't know if he'll be OK to do that.'

She was about to lose her temper. Or her cool. Or something. He could feel it.

'Lewis, I'll do my best. I'll try and make it midday. Look, I have to go.'

Sean took the phone from her hand and set it down beside them. 'He wants your dad to call him?' he asked as neutrally as he could.

'Yes. It's all about Lewis and how busy he is.'

Sean gave a humourless laugh that couldn't hide his disdain for Lewis Earnshaw, and she laughed softly.

'Sometimes it seems . . . ' she began, then stopped abruptly. 'I thought I'd lost Dad, Sean. I thought that was it.' He felt her tremble and he pulled her closer as she began to cry quietly as if she might never stop.

★ ★ ★

The warmth and brightness on her face had woken her and it had taken her several moments to think where it was. To think where she was, actually, because although she was on the sofa, things were different.

She blinked in the sunlight, wondering why the curtains weren't closed, then as she pushed a hand through her hair her fingers touched a drop pearl earring. She was still wearing her earrings, still wearing her silver evening dress.

Well, she'd made an even bigger fool of herself than before and somehow she had to deal with it. Sean had driven her home and reluctantly come in for tea. She'd known he hadn't wanted to, but she'd made it impossible for him to refuse.

Then she'd broken down and he'd comforted her. After he'd left she must have fallen asleep on the sofa.

Staring up at the ceiling, Catherine allowed herself to remember all that had happened the previous evening. That façade she'd been hiding behind for so long had cracked in spectacular fashion and it couldn't have happened in front of a worse person.

Oh, he'd been perfect — he'd comforted her, held her close and made her feel special and cared for. The trouble was that, kind as he'd been,

Sean Radford-Jones was not the sort of man a woman could rely on. He was a free spirit, a loner, almost a drifter who made no secret of the fact that commitment to him was a very dirty word.

And Catherine Earnshaw was in love with him.

How could she not love him? He was the man she'd been waiting for all her life, the one she'd been dreaming of and didn't really believe existed. But he did — and now she had to face him and keep her secret, at all costs. It was bad enough to remember how she'd clung to him but it would be even worse if he realised just why she'd wanted to hold on to him so desperately.

Sean didn't want a relationship — and even if he did she was the last woman he would choose. She knew that instinctively and from everything that had happened since the night they'd met. He was attracted to her — he'd made that very obvious — though she was well aware that part of the attraction had been her own reaction to him and the challenge that represented.

The last thing she could bear was a look of embarrassment or pity in his eyes.

She would have to see him, of course — not only because their paths would inevitably cross through their work, but because he was her father's friend. She would see him in her home, across the dinner table or playing chess with her dad, and she would have to pretend that he meant nothing more to her than a casual acquaintance who'd been there when she needed a bit of sympathy and understanding.

She headed for the bathroom and finally dared to look at herself in a mirror, wincing as she did so. Panda eyes. There was probably mascara all over the cushion too, but she decided not to worry about that until later. Right now she needed a shower, a change of clothes and a cup of coffee. And she needed to find out how her dad was.

She did feel better after the shower and, dressed in jeans and a pink cotton shirt, headed downstairs. She made her phone call, then busied herself tidying the sitting room.

She'd barely noticed it the previous night — no, you're not going to think about last night, she reminded herself sternly — but it bore the signs of the presence of the emergency ambulance crew. She could see where her dad had been taken ill (the papers spread out over the floor near his chair gave that away) and that the paramedics had had to move the small table beside the chair to reach him.

On the floor, close to the table was the scrap on paper on which she'd written her phone number in case he had needed her. Well, he had needed her, but it had been the paramedic who'd called the number . . . eventually.

Pausing for a moment, she thought about her dad in the hospital. He'd been alone when he was taken ill and he'd been so brave. And while he was lying there, hooked up to machines, he'd been concerned about her. She'd seen it in his eyes. But then again, when had he not been concerned about her? He was her dad and she couldn't imagine life without him. Thank heaven she didn't have to.

As she moved the table back into position and straightened the cushions on the chair, she heard a noise at the door. Turning round she saw Sean.

'Feeling better?'

She gasped. 'What are you doing here?' she asked in astonishment.

He was leaning casually in the doorway, dressed in the dark trousers of his suit and white shirt. At his words she had a quick flashback to when he'd surprised her in the kitchen that first night. She swallowed nervously and realised that her heart was pounding.

'I thought you'd gone home. After I — ' she stopped, feeling a blush warm her cheeks.

'After you'd fallen asleep I let myself

out,' he finished for her. 'I'd made a promise to your dad. So after you fell asleep, I figured I'd get a quick couple of hours' sleep back at the caravan and come straight back in case you needed me.'

In case you needed me. She didn't dare think about how much she needed him or even less about the risk of her showing it.

'Well, thank you,' she said tightly, turning her back on him as she moved the cushions yet again. 'I called the hospital. They said Dad had a good night and they're moving him to the specialist unit so they can run some tests. He can have visitors, the nurse told me, anytime today.'

'Great,' he said.

'The cardiologist will be able to confirm it, but they don't think he'll have to be in hospital more than a few days. He can recuperate at home.' Would he notice the slight shake in her voice? She hoped not.

'Even better. So, are you feeling better?'

'Yes, thank you.' She reached out for the newspaper she'd so carefully folded and placed on the table, moving it now to the bookcase nearby.

'Not liking me this morning?'

So he wasn't going to make it easy for her. She turned to face him again. 'I wouldn't say that. You surprised me, that's all. Look, thanks for all your help last night.' She really had to pull herself together, so she took a deep breath. 'I mean, thank you for helping me last night. I'm sorry I made such a fool of myself.'

He didn't move but she had the feeling he didn't like what she'd said. 'I don't recall you making a fool of yourself,' he said eventually. 'You were upset about Bill.'

'Yes, and you were there when I needed some support, for which I'm very grateful. But Dad's on the mend now, as we knew last night, and I shouldn't have let my emotions get the better of me. Nor should I have trespassed on your kindness, or taken up so much of your time.'

Leant against the doorway, arms folded in front of him, he was the very image of relaxed, confident manhood. He gazed at her for a moment then a smile crinkled the corner of his eyes. 'That was a very nice speech. Did you have notes for this one, too?' he drawled.

Notes for a speech, just like at the lifeboat dinner where it all started. A reminder that she couldn't fool him with a surface display of poise and confidence. He knew too much about her — he knew everything about her — and she swallowed nervously at the thought.

'You have all the answers, don't you, Catherine?' he asked after a moment.

She was Catherine again, not Cathy as she'd been last night. It had sounded like a caress on his lips and she should be glad he was no longer using the nickname because the last thing she wanted was for him to touch her heart again. It really was.

'If you want me to get lost you should just say so.'

'I don't want you to get lost!' she flashed, then bit down on her lip. 'Neither do I want to be reminded that I got in such a state and couldn't cope.'

He looked at her steadily. ''Sorry I made such a fool of myself, I shouldn't have let my emotions get the better of me, I shouldn't have trespassed on your kindness'? From where I'm standing you didn't do any of those things, but if it helps you keep your distance then fine, go ahead. Beat yourself up, give yourself a hard time for showing some emotion.' There was a slight edge to his voice now although he gave no other sign of being perturbed. 'Or if it makes you feel better, blame me.'

'That's not what I'm doing! You were exceptional last night, staying when I knew you didn't even want to come into the house. I'm just embarrassed about being so needy.'

'You weren't needy,' he said shortly, then he grinned. 'I'm glad I was exceptional though.'

She felt her cheeks burning. 'I should have said — your support was exceptional.'

'How disappointing,' he said, eyebrows raised once more. 'The first time I get a compliment from you and it's a slip of the tongue. If that's true.'

Not for the first time he had left her speechless and she stared at him helplessly. Finally he moved from the doorway and walked towards her.

It took all her self-control not to back away although he was smiling at her in a way that made her heart race as he took her hands in his and murmured her name.

'Catherine, Catherine, Catherine. Look at you . . . it's great that your dad's doing OK. You go and do what you have to — tell Bill I'll stop by to see him later.' He smiled down at her with gentle amusement. 'Don't worry about last night. You were upset and I'm glad I was here when you needed someone to lean on.'

She remembered only too well how

she'd leaned on him. 'Sean . . . ' Her fingers stirred and he tightened his grip. 'I don't want to argue,' she said flatly.

'I know. I shouldn't tease you. You fell asleep and I left. I can let myself out. I have a key.'

She stared at him.

'Bill gave me a key when he stayed with you in London in the winter. So I could keep an eye on the place.'

There it was. Finally she understood. The friendly neighbourhood social worker, amateur status, keeping company with the retired man and also willing to step in to help the spinster daughter when she needed a date.

She pulled her hands free and walked away without a word. He could dress, lock the house, go away and do whatever he did on Sundays. She couldn't deal with it anymore. She had to get away.

But admit it, the voice inside her head taunted her as she got into the car and put it into gear. You wanted him to say he stayed because of you. Not because of your dad, but because of you.

It was what one of her literary heroes would have done.

Tears pricked her eyes and she bit down on her lip. She wouldn't cry over him — she wouldn't. It was never going to happen. Time to face up to it, she told herself harshly. He may be the romantic hero of your dreams but you're no heroine and this is no Victorian novel. This is real life.

Hearts didn't break. That was just a cliche. She had to focus on her dad getting better again.

The thought of losing her father had terrified her and putting her foot down hard on the accelerator, she drove faster than she normally did, throwing the car into turns on the twisting road to the hospital and braking at the very last moment.

She needed her father — she needed him to be OK, to hear his familiar voice and feel the love that had surrounded her all her life and given her the happiest and most secure of child-hoods.

A good education, a great job and all the designer clothes in the world didn't mean a thing because underneath she was just a lonely and lost little girl who needed her dad. At that moment, all she needed was her dad.

Catherine Reaches A Decision

Sean let himself into the caravan and threw his suit jacket down on to the bench seat in front of the big, wide windows. Sun was streaming through those windows and he screwed up his eyes against the brightness. It didn't match his mood, which was strange because now Bill was going to be OK, there was no reason to feel unsettled, restless, like there was unfinished business somehow.

She'd thrown him out. Catherine had said that she hadn't wanted him to leave but he didn't believe that for a minute. And if he had any sense he'd be relieved she'd given him the brush-off.

It had been fun, flirting with Catherine at the dinner, then events had taken such a serious turn that he'd felt guilty for even thinking that way.

He'd felt her pain over her dad but he'd never imagined that she could be vulnerable in other ways too.

He would never have dreamed she'd fall asleep on the sofa. but it had touched him to see her tear-stained face at rest. He hadn't known what to do — he'd lingered in the shadows for a few moments and decided to go home.

Oh yes, he'd been shocked to find himself feeling like this. It was unlike him to get so involved. He'd always done things alone, his way, and this wasn't like him at all.

Still, it was the least he could do for Bill, he'd told himself. How could he have left his friend's daughter in such circumstances? It was like being part of the lifeboat crew — it was a responsibility that he'd signed up to. It didn't mean any more than that.

His eyes rested on his jacket and he picked it up. It was far too big for her but he'd liked seeing Catherine wearing his jacket, just as he'd liked being able to comfort her.

Even her embarrassment that morning had been touching in a way. She hadn't made a fool of herself, as she'd thought — there hadn't been anything about her he hadn't liked. Not the way she'd spoken, not the way she'd looked, not the way she'd felt.

Oh what the heck.

He flung the jacket away again and ran a hand through his hair, before striding to the shower. It was Sunday — the day of the week that had no real shape or form — and he was free to please himself.

He could, and probably should, spend some time working on the house but he wasn't in the mood. He just didn't feel like even thinking about it, for some reason.

★ ★ ★

In the end he went into the office. It was as good a time as any to look at the structural engineer's report from the retail and office development he

213

was designing on the outskirts of Copenhagen.

Work on the footings had uncovered hitherto unknown problems and he realised he'd have to fly over and sort it out himself. Blast! He didn't need this just before the important Bridby Council meeting when the clifftop conference and community centre plan would be discussed and decided upon.

Immersed in his work, he barely noticed the passage of time until stirrings of hunger forced him out into the June sunshine, mingling with the crowds of holidaymakers and day trippers.

Finding a table in one of the new continental-style cafes springing up around the bay, he ordered panini and sparkling mineral water while he thought about his work and watched the families on the beach. He liked the town in the winter when it was cold and empty, but he also liked the bustle of the holiday season.

He was an incomer himself so he

could hardly object to sharing the pleasure of this pretty place. He liked to travel but he liked coming back to Bridby. He could be himself here among all the strangers, he thought. Alone but not really alone, just as he liked it.

Afterwards, he browsed some of the shops until he found what he was looking for, then walked back up the hill to collect his car. When he arrived at the hospital, he found Bill Earnshaw in a small ward in the cardiac care unit and looking more like his usual self. The elderly man looked pale and tired, but he welcomed his visitor with genuine pleasure.

They chatted for a while, with Sean doing most of the talking to save Bill the effort. He did find out that 'Katie' had been with her father most of the day but had gone back to the cottage to fetch him fresh pyjamas and toiletries.

Of course she'd want to be with her dad — he knew how close they were — but for some reason he didn't want to talk about Catherine with Bill. Instead he found himself telling the old man about the Copenhagen project and the next job — even farther away — for which he'd been invited to submit a design.

He'd been there about half an hour when he heard someone approach the bed. Immediately he knew who it was — he recognised her footfall — and politely he got to his feet wondering what sort of a reception he would receive. Probably not a very warm one.

'Hello, Dad. Sorry I was so long,' Catherine said softly, then she turned to face Sean with a look that was both resentful and unsure. Maybe she expected him to reignite the animosity between them in the sitting room just a few hours earlier. Or to remind her of the very different tensions between them even earlier at the dinner.

'Hi,' he said, trying not to think about which emotion it would be more dangerous to rekindle. Both, probably, he reflected. There was a lesson there somewhere — one Sean Radford-Jones shouldn't have to learn . . .

'Hi.'

Catherine turned back to her dad, trying to pretend everything was all right when everything was as wrong as it could be. If she'd wanted proof that Sean was indifferent to her, here it was, she thought bitterly as she pulled up a chair beside the bed. They might as well have been strangers, so casual was his greeting. She couldn't even be angry at him because it was all her own stupid fault. She was the one who'd fallen in love.

'You've not been long,' Bill Earnshaw said as Sean sat down once more on the other side of the bed. Her dad's voice was weak, but he was looking better. Was it really less than 24 hours ago that he'd collapsed with a searing pain in his chest?

'I've brought your things, Dad,' she said, indicating the bag at her feet and trying not to look at the man seated opposite her.

'Thanks, love.'

'I couldn't leave you here without proper pyjamas, could I? Anyway, how are you feeling?'

'A lot better. I'm thinking it was a lot of fuss about nothing, really. And I spoiled your evening, Katie.'

Her eyes filled with tears. She seemed to have been on the verge of weeping almost all the day and the knowledge that her dad was worrying about her once more instead of his own precarious health threatened to send her over the edge at last. 'Oh, Dad. You didn't spoil anything.'

'Your first proper night out since you've been home . . .'

'You didn't spoil anything,' she repeated softly.

'Your daughter's right,' Sean said unexpectedly. He had stayed silent during their exchange and she could have forgotten he was there if she weren't so aware of every inch of him, every slight breath, every movement. 'You shouldn't be worrying about us because last night wasn't spoiled in any way. It was a perfect night made better by knowing that you're doing fine.'

Catherine felt a shiver down her spine. She knew he was trying to reassure her father — and she was aware he would believe Sean's words when he might not trust his own daughter's — but it didn't help. It really didn't help.

She thought about what Helen Padley had said when she'd called her that morning. She'd begun to tease her about her date with Sean — until Catherine had explained everything that had happened.

'Oh Catherine,' her friend had said with dismay. 'I had no idea about your dad. Is he going to be all right?'

Lost in her thoughts once more, she almost started as Sean stood up and spoke directly to her dad. 'I'll be off then, Bill, now that Catherine's here. You take it easy and I'll see you tomorrow.'

'Thanks for coming, Sean. Thanks

for the crossword book,' he said, and Catherine's eyes were drawn to the slim volume resting on the nightstand. A thoughtful gift from someone who knew her dad very well. 'When do you go on your trip?'

Trip. She didn't know anything about a trip. But then again, she knew nothing about him, not really. He said very little about himself — he was skilful at drawing secrets out of others, herself included, and equally adept at keeping his own life under wraps.

He shrugged and smiled slightly. 'I'm not sure. But I'll come over tomorrow.'

After one last smile at her dad, then a quick nod and a 'see you later' to herself he left them. Despite herself, despite everything she'd told herself, Catherine turned her head to watch as he left the ward.

Except he wasn't leaving — he was standing not so far away in conversation with two nurses who were gazing up at him in fascination and admiration. She shouldn't have been surprised. She'd called him a free spirit and he was.

Resolutely, she turned back to her father and she smiled at him. It was just her and her dad, which was fine. The one man a girl could always rely on was her dad. 'You've got some colour back, you know,' she said encouragingly.

'I'm feeling fine.'

'It's only the first day. It'll take a while to get back to where you were . . . '

'I don't want you fussing over me, Katie.'

'Oh, Dad.'

'Now don't 'oh Dad' me. I'm all right, love. It's lovely that you're here but you can't do this every day. You've got your newspaper to see to.' His voice was weaker than it had been 24 hours earlier, but the strength of character and determination she'd known all her life was still there.

She took his hand in hers. 'They can do without me for a few hours this week. Nobody's indispensable, not even me.'

'I know, but they do need you. Sean was telling me about his work, too,' he murmured, his eyelids flickering as if he were about to drift into sleep. 'So interesting . . . You should go out with him again, Katie. When he gets back from his trip.'

'Maybe,' she said softly. 'I'll call Lewis later to let him know how you are. You can talk to him tomorrow, Dad. The time difference makes it so difficult. He'll understand.'

He moved his head slightly in an attempt at a nod. She watched his face relax and listened to his breathing as he slipped into a deep and untroubled sleep.

You should go out with him again, Katie.

Maybe.

Or maybe not. Watching him with those other women, the pain had been so sharp it was almost physical but perhaps it was for the best. He wouldn't see her later.

When he did see her it would be like

today. He'd be visiting her dad and she would be there in the background. And they would meet through their work, too, but always in the company of other people. What else should she expect? They were nothing to each other.

End of story.

It's Never Too Late For Love

Your dad's home, then?' Catherine settled back into the soft cushions of the sofa and cupped her mug of coffee in her hands. She relished these moments when she could sit and chat with Helen Padley.

Once they'd been teenagers together then their lives had followed very different paths. Helen had married Dave, given up university and brought up a family in the home town she'd sworn she would leave. And Catherine was the flip side of the coin — the successful career girl who'd made it to the top of the tree, achieved the dream . . . and found the pot of gold at the end of the rainbow empty.

She didn't regret all the years away from Bridby — she'd loved her job, loved all the different places, the city life — but somehow there'd always been something missing. Real friends, a family's love and support, a special person ... the one ... She'd come home looking for the missing pieces and she'd found them — in Helen, in her dad and in Sean. But she didn't dare think about Sean so she focussed on the other two instead. The friend she should never have lost touch with and her father, who loved her and needed her.

'Yes, he's doing really well, Helen,' she said slowly, allowing herself a smile as she thought about him. 'When I saw him in the hospital I would never have believed it, but he's made good progress. He's almost back to his old self.'

'I'm glad,' Helen said sincerely, sitting across from her on the other office sofa. 'I like your dad. I always did. I hated to think of him being so ill.'

'I know.' Catherine thought for a moment. Whatever else happened, her dad was still her dad and she wouldn't have him any other way.

'When I think about it, he quite enjoyed being in hospital after the first shock. He hates people fussing over him but he seemed quite comfortable there.'

Her friend smiled widely. 'All those nurses fussing over him — I'll bet he loved it! He's quite the charmer, you know.'

Catherine wrinkled her nose at the mental image Helen's words created. 'My dad?'

'Yes. He has — I don't know — a glint in his eye. I'll bet he's a real hit with the ladies.'

Catherine burst out laughing. 'Please,' she said, struggling with the image even more now. Her dad was the best man she knew, but even so . . . Then a memory stirred — a nice one, one that made her smile.

'Mum always said he was handsome. And he did seem to be getting special treatment from the volunteers who run the hospital library service. One of the ladies goes to Dad's local history class and she was bringing him all sorts of things to read.'

'There you are. He's still got it!' Helen giggled slightly, but behind the laughter in her eyes Catherine could see the concern. 'I'm glad he's feeling better.'

Catherine nodded, then she sighed softly. 'But he's seventy and needs a heart bypass operation. They've put him on the waiting list but it could be months. He needs looking after, Helen.'

'And you're going to do that?'

'That's what I'm here for. I never thought I'd say this but I really like the idea of looking after him. I've been on my own too long.'

'Hmmph! You should try having three kids — that's too many people to look after.'

'I wouldn't mind.'

It was true. She wouldn't mind. In fact . . . Suddenly she wanted someone to care about more than anything. She'd thought about having a family of her own. When she'd been married to Peter — for those few short months before he'd decided he wanted someone else.

It must be coming back to her childhood home, the place of so many happy memories of family life, that was making her yearn for something she felt sure she was missing out on.

'What about the other man in your life? How's Sean?'

Catherine froze. She held the coffee cup to her lips but she didn't move a muscle. It was a subject on which she couldn't be so honest, even with her best friend. Especially with her best friend.

'Fine, I suppose,' she said slowly, trying to think of the best thing to do. This was what she was good at, after all. Making decisions, sifting through the information in front of her, editing it, presenting it in the best possible way.

And in this case that meant not denying that he was 'in her life'. He was — just not as much as she wanted. Not in the permanent, happy-ever-after way.

'Fine? Is that it? Have you been out again?'

For someone who didn't rate her professional abilities very highly Helen was doing a very good impression of a first-rate interviewer who was determined to get to the truth of what instinct told her was quite a story.

'No. The dinner was a one-off.' In every way. There was no chance of happy-ever-after with a man whose idea of commitment was having his mail delivered to his home instead of a post-office box.

And just because she loved him didn't mean Sean had to love her. Real life wasn't like that . . . grown-up women didn't even dare to dream that they might actually 'have it all'.

There was silence for a moment. 'I don't believe you,' Helen said eventually, crossing her arms as she gazed speculatively at her friend. 'You're being too cool. If there was really nothing between you, you'd be sitting down for a good gossip and a chat about what happened, what he said — everything.'

Catherine felt a warmth on her cheeks, but was determined to say nothing. What could she say? *Yes, something did happen. I cried in his arms. Now I'm not sure if I'll ever see him again except as a friend of my dad's, which I know won't touch his heart though it's breaking mine. It's not his fault I've fallen hopelessly in love with him . . .*

She couldn't say any of that — and she just hoped none of it was written on her face.

In London she'd always managed to mask her feelings — it was only since she'd returned to Bridby that all those suppressed emotions had come to the surface.

'I know you,' Helen continued, smiling now, and Catherine wasn't quite sure the other woman wasn't reading her thoughts. 'I remember when we were teenagers. You always said you wouldn't settle for second best. You were waiting for a hero — like the ones we used to read about.'

'You can't compare a teenage dream of a knight on a white charger with . . . ' Her voice tailed off. With what? With Sean?

'I think you've found him.'

Catherine opened her mouth to object but her friend merely smiled at her smugly across the room. 'I know you're my boss and you can sack me if you want — and then I'll really know that I'm right. Think about it, Catherine.'

With that Helen rose and picked up a bundle of papers.

'Meanwhile, life goes on. We need to sort out this article about the clifftop development. It's all very well you having all these brainwaves but I've got to carry them out, Catherine Earnshaw,' she said, matter-of-factly all of a sudden as if they hadn't just been discussing matters of the heart.

They were on safer ground now and Catherine found herself smiling. 'You sound like my dad. It's my 'fancy London ideas' again!'

'It's a good idea — and you know it. The Gazette giving the people of the town their say? This hasn't happened in living memory!'

'It's long overdue.'

'You're telling me. And, Catherine,' Helen paused in the doorway, a glint in her eye. 'And I have a feeling a certain person will be very interested in this particular feature, too!'

* * *

A certain person. Catherine tried to ignore that comment. In fact, she was trying her best to ignore all thoughts of Sean Radford-Jones. But somehow, he found his way into her mind every hour of every day. The problem was that he was everywhere.

Their paths crossed at work and he was her father's friend as well as a colleague of Helen's husband, Dave, in the lifeboat crew. He invaded her dreams too, but she didn't resent that. No way could she forget him — even if she wanted to. And she really would have to be crazy to want to do that. Coming to a decision, she logged out of the computer, tossed some papers into her briefcase and grabbed the jacket of her suit.

'Julie, I'm going home,' she told her secretary as she passed by her desk. 'I'll return any calls tomorrow. I don't think there'll be anything urgent.'

It was a first and she saw the shock on the other woman's face. Catherine Earnshaw, leaving the Gazette office mid-afternoon.

Well, they'd just have to manage without her. She didn't want to be indoors — she wanted to be at home with her dad, a daughter instead of an editor, a normal woman instead of a business leader.

Being a daughter was one role she didn't want to change, though, she reflected as she reached Holly Cottage, her eyes resting on her father as he sat in a garden chair on the lawn, his crossword book in one hand, a pen in the other and a tall glass of lemonade on a table by his side.

The flower beds her mother had tended so lovingly were neglected now, but on a bright May day there was no more welcoming sight than her dad at home in the place they both loved.

'Hello, Katie,' Bill Earnshaw said, looking up at her with a smile

'Hi, Dad. Surprised to see me?' She bent to kiss his forehead, taking in the renewed colour in his cheeks and the brightness of his eyes.

'Yes. it's only . . . ' He glanced down at his watch in puzzlement. 'It's not three o'clock yet. Is everything all right at the newspaper?'

'It's good,' she said easily, returning his smile as she set down her bag and dropped into the empty garden chair beside him. He shouldn't have carried the chairs out on to the lawn, of course, and she started to tell him he was supposed to be resting, but something stopped her. She didn't want to spoil the afternoon by fussing, as he called it. 'That looks good, too,' she said, her gaze resting on the chilled drink in his glass.

'It's lemonade,' he said almost proudly. 'Real lemonade. Not the fizzy stuff.'

'Did we have that in the cupboard?'

'No, Mary brought it,' he said, getting carefully to his feet. Independent and proud, but sensible, too — that was her dad.

She frowned. 'Mary?'

'You saw her at the hospital. She was delivering library books . . . I'll get you a drink. No, love, I can do it. You've been at work and Dr Linden says I have to be active. Mary says so, too.'

Catherine had a flashback to Helen Padley's comments and she smiled as she forced her memory back further to the woman she'd met briefly on the hospital ward. A smallish, plump woman in her late sixties. No blue rinse or twinset, but neat grey hair and a friendly face. Maybe her dad was a charmer after all.

She watched him in amusement as he crossed the lawn towards her, carefully carrying a tray bearing two drinks.

'I'm pleased you're settling in, love,' he said, setting down the glasses and retaking his seat beside her. 'I was worried about you at first. You know, whether you'd made the right decision in coming back here.'

'So was I!' She smiled at him. 'But I haven't regretted it for a minute, Dad. I know I've done the right thing. But anyway, you shouldn't be fretting about me.'

'You don't stop worrying about your children just because they're grown up. You're still my little girl . . . '

'I'm thirty-four!' She didn't feel it. Just occasionally — when she was worried about the newspaper, of the responsibility being the editor entailed — she felt much older than that, but most of the time she still felt 18 inside — still waiting for all the wonders life had to offer, still dreaming, still hoping . . .

'You're still my little girl,' he repeated and after a split second pause he reached out to take her hand. Looking down at their linked fingers, Catherine felt a moment's amusement at the gesture. He wasn't a demonstrative man — she knew her dad loved her and she didn't need actions to prove it.

'Katie, I want to tell you something,' he said quietly and the amusement became concern.

'Are you feeling all right? It's not your heart, is it?'

'Stop worrying, love, I'm fine. No, it's not about that. Mary came over today.'

Catherine nodded. 'With the lemonade. From your history course.'

'That's it. She's a widow. Like me, I suppose. We've been friends for a long time. And the thing is, Katie . . . we want to spend the rest of our lives together. We're going to get a little bungalow.'

She stared at him, unable to process the words because she was sure she must have heard wrongly. Surely her dad hadn't just said that he had a secret lady friend and that he wanted to get married?

'Married?' She repeated the words dumbly because her brain really wasn't functioning at that moment. She heard the sound of birds in the trees and the dull buzz of the traffic on the nearby road but nothing else seemed to make sense. Her dad — whom she had come home to take care of — was telling her he was moving out.

'I can't manage this house,' he was saying, glancing at the building that had been his home for almost 40 years. 'And Mary's sold hers. They've finished some new bungalows for rent along Hornborough Road and we've a chance of one if we're quick.'

Catherine looked down at their intertwined hands, then back up to her Dad's face. He looked slightly tense and there was concern in his eyes but there was something else there, too. Anticipation, excitement about the future. Happiness. When was the last time she'd seen her dad truly happy?

'I'd no idea,' she said softly.

'I know. Katie, it doesn't mean I don't still love your mum . . . And I didn't want to introduce you too soon.'

'Dad, I know that,' she interrupted, the emotion catching in her voice. 'Mum would want you to be happy — I know that. I want you to be happy too.'

He sniffed and said nothing for a moment. When he did speak again his voice was so soft she could barely hear the words. 'I never thought I'd meet somebody else, not at my age. But with the heart attack and everything.'

Her eyes filled with tears. Not much more than a week ago he'd been taken to hospital more dead than alive. He'd had a second chance at life — now he was being offered a second chance at love, too. No wonder he wanted to grasp it. Suddenly she wanted him to grasp it, too, with both hands and hold on tight and never let it go . . .

'I was the one who left home when I was in my teens, remember?' she said with a slow smile. 'Now you're the one who's going to do it!'

He looked at her in sudden concern. 'It's not that I'm not thankful you came home, but, love . . . you shouldn't be looking after an old man at your age. You should have a family of your own.'

'Dad . . . ' The smile wavered.

'I know you'll tell me to mind my own business but — all right, I will mind my own business. But you're all right with this, aren't you, Katie? You'll like Mary — her sons have both moved away and she's been on her own since her husband died.'

'I haven't seen you look so excited about something since . . . well, for years. Of course, I'll like her. I can't wait to meet her properly.'

He smiled and nodded. 'Sean's met her. He did a presentation on his project to her women's club. He doesn't know about us though.'

Catherine knew where she'd got her ability to keep a secret. And along with the knowledge that she'd been living with her dad for weeks now without knowing a thing about him came the ridiculous realisation that her 70-year-old father had a better love life than she did.

She looked across at him, at his lined face and thick glasses, and suddenly she wanted to laugh. 'You old fraud!' she exclaimed. 'You've been having us all on. You weren't interested in local history at all.'

'I am interested . . . '

'No wonder you would never do the homework. You only went to the classes to see Mary.'

'Katie!' he protested but she saw the smile on his lips.

A charmer all right. What woman could resist him?

'Fraud,' she stated as she picked up the glass and took a sip of the lemonade. It was sharp and refreshing but as she gazed down into the cloudy liquid a new thought occurred to her. 'Are you going to sell the cottage?'

'Oh, the cottage.' His smile faded. 'That's the other thing I've got to tell you. Remember when Lewis was home a couple of years ago?'

As if the sun had suddenly disappeared behind a dark, heavy cloud, Catherine felt herself tense. Somehow even the mention of her brother's name could do that.

It wasn't that they didn't get on — it was more that they didn't relate to each other in any way. His neglect of their father was never going to help change that either. She used every ounce of self-control she possessed to keep what she really wanted to say inside, instead saying casually, 'He wanted to buy some property, didn't he? As an investment while he's working in the Middle East?'

She knew what was coming but the knowledge didn't make it any easier to hear.

'Yes, and because I was struggling with this house — I can see it's not what it was — he offered to buy it from me. Now, Katie, he paid me a fair price . . . '

He named the sum and Catherine winced. More like half the market value, she thought in horror, and she bit down hard on her tongue in an effort to stay silent as he continued, 'The arrangement was that I would live here — he's not charging me any rent, and the money is in the bank. I told you I had a savings account, didn't I? He might want to sell the house now, though.'

OK, things really were getting crazy, Catherine thought. Not only was her elderly father fleeing the nest as if he were the child and she the parent, now she was going to be homeless too. But instead of crying she found she wanted to laugh hysterically. Single, homeless and still trying every day to prove herself in a job she'd dreamt of doing since childhood. High-flying Catherine Earnshaw had come down to earth with a bump and the landing was anything but soft. Ouch, ouch and ouch again.

She looked across at her dad, and

saw the worry lines on his face. The last thing she wanted to do was spoil his happiness so she swallowed everything she wanted to say.

'You're right, Dad,' she said with a slow smile, hoping he wouldn't be able to read the truth in her eyes. 'It all works very well. You don't have to worry. Everything's perfect. Absolutely perfect. So tell me about Mary.'

★   ★   ★

Sean looked at the photographs on the walls while he waited to be shown into the office of the editor of the Bridby Gazette. His first visit to her domain, he thought as he studied the image of the abbey at sunset, silhouetted against a cerise and orange sky.

They were good pictures, and he nodded slightly as he read the name underneath each view. Neil Mitchell. Catherine always gave credit where it was due and she was confident and generous enough to want to encourage talent rather than plunder it for her own benefit.

He'd barely seen her since Bill left hospital. Since she'd dumped him so unceremoniously the morning after that night before, Catherine had been avoiding him. It wasn't easy in this small town but somehow she'd managed it. Not that he'd expected to see her at the cottage the previous evening. She'd always worked late on Thursdays and that was one of the reasons he and Bill Earnshaw had chosen that day for their weekly chess game.

It had been good to see Bill back home and looking so much better. They'd fallen back into old habits and chatted easily as they played a game that for all its friendliness was highly competitive. He'd been there about an hour when the older man spoke into the silence as they each studied their next move.

'Katie's upset.'

That had wiped the smile off his face, Sean remembered. He didn't like to think of her being hurt. They were friends, after all.

He rested his hand on his rook and spoke carefully. 'About your plans to get married to Mary?'

'Oh, no. She's been lovely about that. No, it's . . .'

He looked up into his friend's troubled face and waited. It wasn't up to him to force a confidence from Bill about his daughter — however much he wanted to hear it.

Eventually Bill spoke again. 'No, you see, I've done something very silly . . .'

You couldn't argue with that, Sean thought as he gazed at the photograph of the abbey without seeing it. He could understand her feelings about it, too — even if he couldn't understand how a brother and sister could be so different.

★ ★ ★

You're here for the meeting, too?' He started and turned quickly, finding himself face to face with a man in a business suit whose face he vaguely recognised but whose name he couldn't remember for the life of him. He nodded and half-smiled, ignoring the resentment inside him that this wasn't going to be a one-on-one encounter with Catherine. Like he was expecting it to be . . .

Minutes later he was sitting at a round conference table in her office, two men on his left, one on his right and Catherine seated opposite him. She was the only woman in the room but that didn't seem to faze her. Not that it should, of course. She knew what she was doing — she'd always known what she was doing.

She was every inch the business-like editor today, he thought, taking in the stylish but understated trouser suit. Her hair was held back at the nape of her neck so there was nothing — no unconscious gesture — to give away signs of discomfort or nerves. Nor was there a trace of the vulnerable woman clutching his hand in the hospital, or even less the beautiful creature from the lifeboat dinner, looking deep into his eyes.

He looked down at the agenda in front of him and tried to switch his mind to the subject of the proposed arts festival. Why he'd been asked to sit on this committee he didn't know — heaven knew he was too busy with his own work — but somehow it had happened so he had better get his mind on the job in hand. Like Catherine was doing.

The meeting moved along briskly. She was an efficient chairwoman and within an hour they'd made the progress they'd expected to and more. But when the others began to head towards the door he made no move to follow them. As their voices faded away, Catherine looked up from the discarded papers she was gathering and she seemed to see him properly for the first time.

'Are you all right?' he asked softly and immediately wondered why he had.

'Did I do so badly in the meeting?' she asked mildly.

'I spoke to Bill,' he said and the flush

on her face deepened. She looked uncomfortable and troubled, the veneer of calm efficiency shattered by his quiet words.

'He told you, I suppose — about selling the house?' He nodded and she sighed. 'I can't believe Lewis would do that to Dad.'

'You know what I think about your brother.'

Something flickered in her eyes — maybe the memory of the last time they'd spoken of the absent Lewis Earnshaw. He'd been holding her so close at that moment that he could feel her heart beating underneath the flimsy dress.

'He's never cared a fig about anyone or anything except himself,' she stated, then she sighed again. 'No, that's not fair. He does care about Dad, but . . . did he tell you what Lewis paid for the cottage?'

She mentioned a figure and Sean let out a low whistle. 'I could do with your brother as my accountant. He'd save me a fortune,' he commented and to his surprise Catherine almost smiled.

'Yes. Well, he's very smart. I know Dad couldn't manage the place and nobody knew I was coming home then. But the house was meant to be Dad's insurance policy. He doesn't have a very big pension and there was always the house if he needed to pay for care. And now that's gone — or half of it has, at least.'

'I know,' he said quietly. 'Is there anything I can do?'

He stretched out a hand as if to touch hers but somehow it never reached its destination and Catherine turned to gaze out of the window across the bay. 'Go over to Dubai and talk some sense into my brother?' she said, then shrugged and sighed again. 'Actually, I may go and do that myself.'

That made him smile. In a battle between the lowlife brother and Catherine he knew who he'd pick as the winner . . . 'Now why can I imagine you doing that? Look, you'll always be there to watch out for your dad, Catherine.

He knows that.'

She was silent for a moment, then she smiled at him — one of those rare, genuine smiles that transformed her whole face. 'I've never seen him happier. Mary's lovely and they've got so many plans. I'm the one with nowhere to go. You're not planning to build any flats, are you? If you are I'll be interested.'

He shook his head slowly. 'I can't help you there. The only house I've ever designed is my own.'

She drew in a sharp breath then fell silent for a moment, and he waited patiently for her next words. When they came her voice was flat and unemotional. 'Of course. Of course it is.'

Now what was all that about? Had his answer disappointed her in some way, did she want him to say something else? Sean thought for a moment. 'I told Bill I'd help move his stuff to the new place. I have to go away but I'll be back in time.'

'Dad said you were going on a trip. I hope you get everything sorted out.'

Why not come with me?

He didn't say the words out loud but the thought was there in his mind. It came from nowhere and it shocked him because it was the last thing Sean Radford-Jones would ever think or do. Take a woman on a business trip with him? Take Catherine?

He always travelled alone. Always. It meant he could do exactly what he wanted, when he wanted. It suited him — he liked being alone and there was nothing or no-one to make him want to change that, was there? Was there?

Catherine would like Copenhagen, he knew that, and it would do her good to have a break. He could imagine himself showing her the designs for the project, too — she'd have an opinion on them to be sure and she would be certain to tell him what that opinion was . . . Then when his work was done they could see the city together — something he'd never had the time or inclination to do alone — discovering its fabled treasures, exploring its hidden corners . . .

Come with me. He could have said it, but it was a crazy idea so he didn't. Instead he watched her pick up the papers from the table and slip them into a clear plastic folder which she held against her chest. He didn't need a body language expert to tell him what that gesture meant.

'I expect you need to go.'

'Not really. I . . . '

'Excuse me, Catherine.' It was her secretary — the newspaper's editorial secretary — hovering in the office doorway, her gaze flicking from one to the other then back again. 'Mr Janner is here, from the Traders' Association.'

'He's early,' Catherine said flatly.

The man was probably keen. Sean couldn't blame him. 'It's all right, I'm going,' he said grabbing his own briefcase. He glanced at the secretary, then at Catherine. 'I'll see you later,' he said briefly then made his escape.

He didn't slow his pace until he stepped out into the fresh air of the harbourside when he paused and drew in a deep breath. Not just an escape — a lucky escape. Any longer in that office and he really might have done something crazy. Like say the words out loud. Oh boy . . .

He really needed to get away — from too much emotion and too much temptation to go out on a limb in a way he never had before. Sure, he found Catherine attractive, who wouldn't, and she'd been good company that day on the beach, and even more so at the dinner.

But she was his friend's daughter and he'd been helping her out, nothing more. Anything more would be playing with fire. And even as he vowed not to think about her while he was on his trip, his brain was reminding him that when you played with fire you got burnt.

He needed to keep his distance, take care of himself and go his own way. The way it has always been. The way it will be.

A Tense Meeting With Sean

Sean didn't understand it as he threw a few things into a holdall and drove to the airport. He didn't understand it on the flight when he avoided conversation with everybody — fellow passengers and pretty flight attendants alike — or in Copenhagen when he finally arrived with a whole lot of work to do and problems to sort out . . .

For some reason he couldn't stop thinking about Catherine, what had happened between them and how good it had felt to kiss her, hold her, watch her smile . . . There was a nagging ache inside him that he couldn't identify — and didn't dare try.

He didn't know what it was but he was restless, struggling to concentrate on his work during the day and returning to his hotel room early each evening on the pretext of having more work to do. Except he never did it. He brooded and wondered, then berated himself before starting all over again.

Nothing helped. Especially not the link to the online edition of the Bridby Gazette, emailed over by his ever-efficient secretary. He stared at the website as he sat at his makeshift desk in the site office and thought not about the soft, vulnerable woman this time, but the other Catherine Earnshaw. The professional one, the editor who instead of getting a reporter's view or that of an expert on his developments had given that section of the paper over to the people who truly mattered — the residents of Bridby.

Four of them — a teenager, a young mother, a middle-aged teacher and a retired fisherman — had all researched and analysed his cliff-top project. Then they'd given their verdicts. For once it wasn't all PR or cynical journalism — just honest views, sometimes critical, sometimes praising, which all concluded that the development would benefit the people of the town. Not its planners or its dignitaries, but its people . . .

He'd always known Catherine was good — he hadn't needed to see today's paper to appreciate that — but seeing it in full colour struck a chord somewhere inside him. He read the articles again, each and every one, then picked up the phone.

As he waited he looked at the illustration on the pages . . . A computer-generated image of how the town would look with the development perched high on the cliff, above the harbour, across from the abbey and the Norman church. A familiar scene — one he saw every day . . . Suddenly he didn't want to spoil that scene. He wanted to enhance it.

'Colin?' he said at the sound of his assistant's nervous voice at the other end of the line. He was a good architect, the younger man, but he needed help and guidance to become a really good one . . .

'Sean, is everything OK?'.

'It's fine. Listen. I'm going to make a few calls from here, but I need you to do something at your end. I want you to call the council and tell them we're putting in a revised planning application.'

The young man's voice was laced with puzzlement. 'But they've told us it will be approved. Even the Gazette — well, even the people in the Gazette support it.'

'There's nothing that can't be improved. We're going to use local stone for the façade, Colin. Yeah, I know, but we'll cover the cost. This is what I need you to do . . . '

He'd always trusted his instincts when it came to his work and he knew he was doing the right thing. He knew it five days later when he walked into the council chambers for the meeting that would decide on the application. He was able to greet everyone casually and calmly while his gaze scoured the room for a certain brunette, but try as he might he couldn't see her. She wasn't there. He couldn't believe it — she wasn't there.

'Hi, Sean. Have you jetted in specially for the meeting?'

He found himself face-to-face with Helen Padley and smiled. He liked her, he really did, and suddenly he was glad to be back in Bridby.

'Hey,' he said, bending to brush her cheek with his lips. 'Great to see you.'

'Thanks. It's all very exciting, isn't it?'

'Yeah, exciting. So long as they say yes. So . . . no Cathy tonight?' He hadn't intended to say that. Especially not to Helen who had the heart and soul of a matchmaker. And he definitely had not intended to refer to her as Cathy. Nobody called her that.

'She's helping her dad — getting ready for his big move on Saturday,' Helen answered with a gleam in her eye. 'I thought you'd know that.'

'I know Bill and Mary are moving, sure.' He'd intended to help out with

Bill's move into his bungalow — the last thing his elderly friend needed after his heart attack was to over-exert himself — but he had to fly back to Denmark after the meeting. This job . . . sometimes he could almost hate it.

'They have tons of stuff to sort through,' Helen was saying. 'They've lived in that house as long as I can remember. But Catherine says this is my project anyway and I should see it through, so here I am. We all know the development's going to be approved and quite right too. It'll transform our town.'

He looked at her. 'For the right reasons, I hope,' he said seriously.

'Jobs, revenue, a high profile. And it's going to look beautiful, too. What's not to love?'

He was the wrong person to ask. He'd always been passionate about the development and he wanted other people to be, too. Awards and accolades were fine but he wanted to see this project come to life, be buzzing with activity and a centre of the community. He thought about that as he walked up to the cluster of small bungalows not far from the harbour on Saturday afternoon. He didn't just want to design it, to create something then walk away. He wanted to stay and see it flourish. He wanted to stay.

The first thing he saw when he walked into the central courtyard was Catherine, carrying a large terracotta tub of flowers which she set down outside the entrance to the bungalows.

She was dressed in shorts and a sleeveless T-shirt and he just knew that if he looked closely her hands would be dirty from her work. She wasn't a woman who held back — whatever she did, she did it wholeheartedly. He knew that.

She dropped to her knees and began to pat down the soil around the plants, every so often raising a hand to push her hair out the way. She'd allowed it to grow slightly and it now reached just beyond her chin. It looked good, he decided as he walked towards her.

'Have I missed all the work?'

She hadn't heard his approach and she was staring as if she'd never seen him before. Or maybe as if she was trying to see inside him, or read his mind. And if she did?

'Hi,' she said eventually, tearing her gaze away from his and dropping it to the plant pot in front of her. 'I didn't expect to see you.'

OK, he hadn't expected Catherine to throw her arms around him but he wanted something more than those cool, dismissive words and he frowned slightly. 'I told your dad I'd be back Saturday. Didn't he say?' he asked casually.

'Well, yes.' She scrambled to her feet — he didn't even offer a hand to help her because he knew she'd refuse it — and brushed the excess soil off her hands before wiping them on her shorts.

'Dad said you were coming back today but I didn't think . . . ' she was saying and he dragged his gaze back to her face. 'You missed the guys with the van — they were wonderful, by the way.'

'They're good guys — they've helped me a lot on the house.'

'Well, look who's here!'

Bill Earnshaw stepped outside the door, a smile of real pleasure on his lined face as he offered a hand for his friend to shake.

'Hello, Sean. Have you come here straight from the airport?'

'Almost. Hey, Bill.' He took the offered hand and shook it warmly, taking in the restored colour in the old man's cheeks and the ease of his breathing, before turning to the woman who had appeared behind him. 'Hello, Mary.'

'You must be exhausted!' she said in concern. With her two sons grown up and moved away, he had a feeling Mary Sweetman would take any and every opportunity to mother him. 'I'll put the kettle on.'

'Catherine's been telling me that I've missed the hard work. But I figure there's more to do. Moving furniture, hanging pictures, whatever — I'm at your service.'

'The energy of the young!' Mary exclaimed laying a hand on his arm affectionately. 'It's Saturday night — don't you have anything else to do instead of running around after us old folk?'

He shook his head. 'I'm on call for the lifeboat. Which I can do here as well as anywhere.'

'You do so much for me,' Bill said with a frown. 'I wish there was something I could do for you.'

He smiled and said with false ease, 'How about that cup of tea? Then tell me where you want me to begin.'

Then Catherine spoke, calm and measured. 'Now you've got more help, I think I'll be off, Dad. There's all the things we brought down from the attic the other day to sort through. I'll make a start and figure out whose it all is — yours, mine or Lewis's.'

Bill looked concerned. 'You're not staying for tea, love?'

Never mind a journalist, she could have been an actress, Catherine told herself, smiling at her father as if she didn't have a care in the world. As if. When she'd looked up to see Sean looming over her she'd thought she might faint at his feet.

Once again he was invading her territory, teasing her with his overwhelming presence, setting her pulses racing while her head painfully reminded her wayward heart that it had no right to beat that way. No right at all.

'No, I don't think so,' she said reassuringly. 'I'll get something at home. I think I've earned a glass of wine at least, don't you? I'm not on call!'

Her dad smiled, as she'd meant him to. 'If you're sure . . . But be careful if you go into the attic by yourself, Katie. You know how funny the ladder is.'

'I will — I promise.'

'If you need anything, give me a call,' Sean said, and she was forced to look at him once again. 'I can go into the attic for you.'

Forced? She liked nothing more than looking at him, except maybe listening to him. She'd forgotten how much she liked his voice. And the way one corner of his mouth tilted upward when he smiled and how when he thrust his hands into his pockets it didn't make him slouch but seem even more superbly formed, accentuating his tall, powerful physique.

'Thank you, but I'll be OK. I'm sure you'll have enough to do. They're very good at delegating the rotten jobs.'

'Thanks for the warning!'

She kissed her dad and then Mary, who smiled and hugged her warmly, before hesitating slightly as she remembered something.

'Congratulations on the project,' she said to Sean almost shyly. She couldn't believe she hadn't already said it. Not when it mattered so much. So, so much . . . 'I like the new design.'

'So do I.'

'It will mean a lot to the people employed in the quarry at Lindley Beck, too. Using local stone, that is.'

'Yeah. I know.' His voice was quiet but he was smiling and Catherine couldn't help responding. She'd once told him she didn't want to fight and it was true. She cared about him too much to reject anything he had to offer, even if it was only friendship.

★ ★ ★

He looked tired, she thought as she let herself into Holly Cottage a few minutes later. He'd been working so hard — Helen had told her that — and now he'd rushed over from the airport to help her father. As Bill had said, he did so much for him and asked for nothing in return.

She stopped and hesitated for a moment instead of closing the door behind her. Perhaps she should go back and help out. There was much she could do, but then again . . . Maybe he wouldn't want her to go back and she couldn't risk it, couldn't risk him guessing how she felt.

No, she'd stay where she was. Soon she'd be moving out of this house, too, and she had to sort through a lifetime's worth of stuff that hadn't seen the light of day for years.

They'd managed to live their lives without it — she, Lewis and their father — yet almost everything she found was full of memories and her progress was slow.

She had no idea her parents had squirrelled so much away and among the boxes of unwanted Christmas decorations and old clothes were some things that she knew she would never be able to part with.

Like her old school books. Shuffling her position, she flicked through the battered old notebooks — seeking out the most important ones in her eyes . . . her favourite subject — English. Here they were, four dark blue books in which the teenage Catherine Earnshaw had poured her heart and soul. Her creative writing . . .

Sitting down on the window seat in her bedroom, she hesitated for a moment. First she'd help herself to that glass of wine she'd promised herself earlier. OK, it was her first night by herself in the old house which wasn't really anything to celebrate but she'd get used to living alone again.

Love Will Always Win

When Catherine opened the fridge her eyes rested on the bottle of champagne she'd bought to take over to the bungalow and had forgotten in the chaos and confusion of the move. She'd do that tomorrow, she decided. Celebrate her dad and Mary's new marriage and no doubt empty a few boxes or assemble some flat-packed furniture, too.

Pouring herself a cup of coffee, she picked up the phone and punched in a number she had committed to heart just hours earlier. She heard it ring and ring — maybe they couldn't find the receiver — then someone answered.

'Hi, Dad. It's me,' she said brightly, feeling like a fretful mother hen. 'How are you getting on?'

'Hello, love,' said that familiar voice. 'Mary's tired but we're all right. Sean's just left — the lifeboat's been called out.'

Her dad was OK but still the earth rocked beneath Catherine's feet. Her eyes were drawn to the kitchen window and the grey clouds beyond. Darkness was closing in but it wasn't nightfall — it was a storm and rain was already rattling against the glass. There was nothing worse than a summer storm at sea — and Sean was out in the lifeboat. 'An emergency?' she asked with false calm.

'A drifting boat, I think. Sean said it would probably be someone just outside the harbour and they'd be back on shore in a few minutes.'

She didn't believe it for a moment, as much she wanted to. Sean had said that to reassure her father, but she wasn't so easily satisfied. He was out in the lifeboat in a storm — and there was nothing she could do about it.

Somehow she managed to get through the call and the moment her dad hung up she punched in another number — the one for enquiries. Within seconds she had what she wanted and was through to the Coastguard station.

'Jim,' she said urgently in a voice that didn't sound like her own. 'It's Catherine Earnshaw, from the Gazette. Is the lifeboat out?'

'Yes, she was launched about fifteen minutes ago, Catherine,' the man said easily. 'We've had reports of a boat in trouble off Ravensea Head.'

'How far off?'

'Twenty miles or so. They'll be out a few hours, I imagine. I was saying that to Sean Radford-Jones — he's the coxswain tonight.'

'I know,' she murmured, closing her eyes.

He was out in the lifeboat in a storm — and there was nothing she could do about it.

Not only out in the lifeboat, but far out at sea. There was a flash of lightning followed by an almost-immediate a clap of thunder, and she shuddered as she thought about the lifeboat and its crew. Most of the callouts were in good weather — people getting stranded, boats breaking down — but the worst cases were when the weather was bad and people were really in trouble.

Going back to her room, she picked up the schoolbooks, but they couldn't hold her attention now. Silly, girlish fantasies . . . She'd sat on this window seat, reading her novels, writing her own stories and dreaming that one day she'd be swept off her feet by a dashing, brooding Heathcliff or Mr Rochester.

But she didn't want a storybook hero anymore. She wanted a real one — the one who'd been right in front of her all the time. Her eyes filled with tears as she thought about him and what he was doing right then.

Who was more of a hero than Sean? He was everything — look how kind he was to her dad, and how he'd been there when she needed him too.

She wanted to cry, but then again she didn't because if he could risk his life in that way the least she could do was have faith in him.

Risk. She almost laughed at her own

thoughts earlier in the evening — the 'risk' of him finding out how she felt. She'd give anything now to be able to tell him how she felt.

Suddenly she remembered something from long ago now abandoned in the attic. A shortwave radio of Lewis's which she could tune in to listen to the Coastguard. And the emergency services if she needed to.

Pulling down the folding ladder to the attic, she heard her dad's warning from earlier. She hesitated, then tested it with one foot. It seemed safe enough and the radio was up there somewhere.

Tentatively she took one step at a time, Sean's offer to help echoing in her mind. A real-life hero . . . her real-life hero . . .

There was so much stuff up there and in the dim light from the single bulb she had to search box after box before she found it. But eventually she had it in her hands and, abandoning all thought of the family possessions she was meant to be sorting through, she headed back down the ladder and into her bedroom. A room where his presence still lingered.

It was an old radio and the signal wasn't very good inside the thick walls of the cottage, but she could just about make out the voices as she sat there on the window seat where he'd held her so close, watching the rain stream down the windows and counting the second between each bolt of lightning and rumble of thunder.

She tried to read but couldn't and eventually she took a long, slow bath as she listened to endless conversations on the radio that didn't seem to tell her anything.

Still restless when she returned to the window seat, she picked up a bottle of nail polish but her fingers didn't seem to work properly and end result would have been disappointing if she'd cared at all.

Eventually — she had no idea how long she'd been listening — a distant voice announced that everybody was onboard and they were heading back to port. Suddenly the world seemed a better place, until the voice said something about notifying the hospital. Someone was hurt . . . Chewing on a newly painted fingernail, she wondered whether to call the Coastguard again. She wanted to know — she had to know . . .

'Are they all OK?' she asked urgently when Jim Pike answered the phone.

'All but one.'

From relief to despair again. No, no, no . . . 'Jim . . . ' she whispered, her voice choked as she waited for the news — any news, just so long as she knew.

'Young Danny Pierce has hurt his arm. It was crushed between the lifeboat and the yacht. It's pretty bad. Sean said they struggled to get him back on board.'

'Sean . . . ' She swallowed nervously. 'Is he OK?'

'In need of a whisky but otherwise fine, he said. Don't worry, Catherine. He's a fine boatman — he'll get his crew home safely.'

Of course he would, she thought with a shuddering sigh. No-one knew better than she how he took care of everybody he knew. Finally, admitting her tiredness and helplessness, she went to bed only to lie awake staring at the window in anticipation of the dawn as she thought about him — safe after his ordeal. At least he was safe — and she would see him again . . .

Eventually she must have fallen into a fitful sleep because the next thing she knew was that it was light. Pulling herself upright, she glanced at the clock . . . almost five . . . then wandered over to the window. Beyond the curtains, a new world had dawned. The sun was rising over the sea into a sky that was clear and fresh. There was a dampness in the air but otherwise no sign of the storm the night before. But somebody would bear the scars.

She showered and pulled on her oldest jeans and favourite sweater, running a brush through her hair quickly but not bothering with make-up. She didn't bother with the car either, walking briskly towards his house through the quiet streets of a town not yet awake. All was quiet at his house, too. His car was there but there was no sign of him. Through the caravan windows she could see that the caravan was empty and the bed not even slept in.

It was easy to find him in the end. She followed the footprints on the beach where the tide had gone out, tracing his steps to the headland where they'd met once before.

He was even sitting on the same rock, looking drawn and pale as he gazed out to sea lost in thought. She watched him for a moment as he'd watched her the previous day until eventually she could stay silent no longer.

'Hey.'

His head turned sharply and his eyes widened at the sight of her as if he couldn't believe she'd sought him out. Then his lips parted in what might have been the beginnings of a smile as the realisation that she had come looking for him set in. 'Hey there,' he said.

'It's early in the day for a walk.'

He shrugged. 'Early or late, I don't know what it is.'

She knew, then, where he'd been while she was trying not very successfully to sleep.

To the hospital with Danny Pierce. Somehow she knew that, just as she'd known he would instinctively seek out that lonely, wild part of the beach from where he took his inspiration as well as his comfort.

Tearing her eyes away from his face she sat down on the rock beside him. 'I don't, either.'

Her gaze swept the bay from the headland beyond to the abbey standing proud and tall on the cliffs as she waited for him to speak. When he did his voice was soft and low. 'I found these for you.'

He opened his hand to show her four fragments of rock, the unique Bridby stone she'd collected as a child. He knew that — she'd told him so that other time they'd met in this place — and she fingered the fragments one by one.

'This is the biggest piece I've ever seen.'

'There's many of them out there on the shoreline, washed up in the storm last night.'

The open sea in front of them was calm, benign and a deep blue in the crystal light of the early morning. 'You wouldn't think,' she said slowly, 'when you look at it now, that it could change so much in no time at all.'

She took the scraps of rock from him and slipped them into her jeans pocket. As she did so, he took her other hand and held it in his warm one.

'That's what catches people out.'

The ends of his fingers were roughened slightly in places from the manual work he did, but they were smooth, too. 'They only see the calm surface — not the hidden dangers. And that it's not just themselves they put at risk.'

He was silent for a moment. 'You've heard?'

She nodded. 'I was listening on a shortwave radio I found in the attic'

'So you know Danny Pierce was injured. Nearly killed . . . '

She turned to look at him, his profile carved like granite against the morning sunlight. 'But he wasn't.'

'He was injured. He may lose his arm. I should have been more careful. It was my watch.'

'You couldn't have done anymore,' she interrupted. 'I talked to the Coastguard. It's a miracle no-one else was injured — and more seriously.'

He looked at her then and there was a flicker of warmth in those troubled eyes. 'You talked to the Coastguard?' he said slowly.

'I'm a journalist — I like to know what's going on.'

'Yeah, that's you. The editor of the Gazette.' He lifted her hand in his own and turned it one way, then the other almost as if he were seeing it for the first time. When he spoke again his voice was a mere whisper, but the strain and worry gone. 'You painted your nails, that's not like you.'

Catherine was sure she was trembling and that he must feel it, but she didn't care. 'It was something to do, while I waited.' *For you*. She didn't say the extra two words but they were there between them as clearly as if she'd shouted them from the rooftops.

'This one's smudged. And this one . . .'

'I couldn't concentrate.'

He continued his examination of her hands for a moment, then raised his head to look at her. 'Will you stay with me?' he asked quietly, fixing her with that intense blue gaze.

She stared at him, drinking in every detail — the softness in his eyes, the warmth of his hand — and she tried to form an answer to his question. 'Yes.' Her voice was surprisingly strong considering that question had almost driven the breath from her body. Strong and sure — very, very sure.

He started to smile. 'Yes? Is that all?' he teased gently. 'You always have something to say about everything. It's one of the things I love about you . . . '

She thought about it for a moment. 'Yes, please?'

Now he laughed. 'Cathy Earnshaw, I'll expect this is the first and only time in the next fifty years that I'll have you lost for words.'

All her life had been leading up to this moment, Catherine realised, to being in this place, with him, looking forward to the next fifty years of living with and loving this man — this amazing, remarkable, strong, gentle, good man. She could hardly believe it except that Sean was smiling at her, holding her close, making her part of him in every way, making her complete. Giving himself to her as she was giving herself to him.

'I want to live with you more than anything else in the world,' she said eventually, daring to return his smile, knowing now that it was real. And that it was for keeps.

'Then you've got it.'

When he rested his lips on hers it was the most romantic thing she had ever known. Not because of the passion of the kiss for it was gentle and soft. No, it was because it was more than just a kiss. It was a promise for the future that bound them to each other in a way more powerful than words ever could be.

'I always wanted someone to take care of,' he said when he pulled back slightly. 'And I always wanted someone to take care of me.'

'You need to sleep,' she said suddenly, getting to her feet and pulling him with her. She didn't want to let go of him at all — not even for a second — now that she knew he needed her as much as she needed him.

★   ★   ★

'I'll never be able to finish this meal if you keep looking at me,' Catherine said. She felt his arms tighten around her as she turned over the bacon in the pan. She felt wonderful. Not tired or worried or afraid any more — just wonderful . . .

'I'm not sure I want breakfast,' he said laughing.

'Now he tells me,' she complained softly, but when she set down the plate in front of him, he ate it with the energy of a man for whom life was good. Very good.

'I think I'm going to like taking care of you,' she said and they smiled at each other. Life was so good all she wanted to do was to say . . . 'I love you.'

His eyes darkened and he sat back in his chair. 'Come here,' he said softly.

She settled herself beside him and felt another deep thrill as his arms closed about her once more.

'There's too much to think about,' he said.

'Mmm, I don't want to think at all. I forget everything when I'm with you.'

'That's the idea!' He laughed softly

and tightened his hold. 'I've been thinking about the future.'

'You can't change your mind now!' She could say that because she knew it wasn't true. He'd told her so when they'd got back to the privacy of the cottage.

'I'll never let you go,' he'd whispered gently in her ear. 'I can't exist without you. You're my reason for being alive. I think we should get married.'

Catherine let out a deep breath. She picked up one of his hands and pressed her lips to the palm.

'Oh yes,' she breathed, then she smiled as she snuggled even deeper into his arms. 'I know your game. You just want to be married to the editor of the Gazette. You have a thing about that.'

'I have a thing about you. But being married to the most important woman in Bridby could be useful. Everybody would have to be nice to me.'

She turned her head and he immediately kissed her lips.

'Sean, everybody in this town is falling over themselves to be nice to you,' she said eventually. 'I'm the only one who wasn't. That's how all this started, remember?'

'I remember everything about you. But anyway, don't you think your dad would want to walk you down the aisle?'

Her dad. She'd almost forgotten her dad over the past few hours! She would have to call him — later of course and tell him their news. 'Give me away you mean?'

'He already did that — to me. I must remember to thank Bill.' He lifted a strand of hair behind her ear and kissed the soft skin. 'For his difficult . . .'

'Yes . . .'

He turned her face towards him and gazed directly into her eyes.

'Impossible . . .'

'Oh . . .'

'Infuriating . . .'

'Sean!'

He brushed her cheek. 'Difficult, impossibly, infuriatingly gorgeous daughter.'

She'd known nothing till she'd met Sean. Nothing.

'You can't tell him that,' she murmured as he held her hands in his.

'Say yes, Cathy.'

'Sean . . . '

'Say yes.'

He had all the power in the world
over her and he knew it. 'On one
condition.'

'Hmmm?' He smiled at her while his
hand grasped hers, intertwining their
fingers as if they could never be parted.
Then she raised that hand to her lips
once more.

'That when the house is finished we
can plant a beautiful garden with grass
and trees and flowers, and you'll have
somewhere wonderful to come home to.'

And listening to her soft voice and
feeling the warmth of her body in his
arms at last, Sean knew that he, too,
had finally come home.

★　★　★

Bridby Gazette, September 18th edition
There were two notable absentees

from Wednesday's long-awaited opening ceremony for the Bridby Abbey Conference, Creative Industry and Community Centre. Architect Sean Radford-Jones, the man behind the award-winning project, had to cancel at the last minute — but with very good reason.

His wife, Catherine Radford-Jones, the Gazette's very own editor, was bringing their first child into the world. We have it on very good authority that 71b 2oz Ben William arrived at exactly the moment the mayor was cutting the tape and declaring the centre open.

We have also been told that Ben has already provided the inspiration for his father's next project — rumoured to be a children's library and play centre. We wish the new family all the best of luck!

THE END

We do hope that you have enjoyed reading this large print book.

Did you know that all of our titles are available for purchase?

We publish a wide range of high quality large print books including:
Romances, Mysteries, Classics
General Fiction
Non Fiction and Westerns

Special interest titles available in large print are:
The Little Oxford Dictionary
Music Book, Song Book
Hymn Book, Service Book

Also available from us courtesy of Oxford University Press:
Young Readers' Dictionary
(large print edition)
Young Readers' Thesaurus
(large print edition)

For further information or a free brochure, please contact us at:
Ulverscroft Large Print Books Ltd.,
The Green, Bradgate Road, Anstey,
Leicester, LE7 7FU, England.
Tel: (00 44) 0116 236 4325
Fax: (00 44) 0116 234 0205